"You think the shooters are gone?

Can we stand up?" Tanya asked. What she wanted to do was get Danny out of the chilly air, get him water, and have him sit down and rest. She still hadn't seen his wound. It could be worse than he thought.

"Stay down," Danny said.

Tanya heard the wail of sirens. Help was almost here. Finally.

"Move your hand away from your neck and let me see your injury," she said to Danny.

He grinned. "Why? Are you worried about me?"

She rolled her eyes. Then she heard the crack of gunfire. A bullet tore a hole in the car to her right, barely missing her. She and Danny dived back toward the asphalt.

Then she heard the growl of an engine as a car accelerated. The gunmen must have circled back after they'd initially sped away. The shooter must have gotten out of the car and sneaked up to the parking lot on foot.

The criminals' determination was fierce, and there was no denying that now Tanya was their target.

Jenna Night comes from a family of Southern-born natural storytellers. Her parents were avid readers and the house was always filled with books. No wonder she grew up wanting to tell her own stories. She's lived on both coasts but currently resides in the Inland Northwest, where she's astonished by the occasional glimpse of a moose, a herd of elk or a soaring eagle.

Visit the Author Profile page at LoveInspired.com.

ABDUCTION IN THE DARK

JENNA NIGHT

LOVE INSPIRED SUSPENSE
INSPIRATIONAL ROMANCE

LOVE INSPIRED® SUSPENSE
INSPIRATIONAL ROMANCE

ISBN-13: 978-1-335-73610-9

Abduction in the Dark

Love Inspired
22 Adelaide St. West, 41st Floor
Toronto, Ontario M5H 4E3, Canada
www.LoveInspired.com

Printed in U.S.A.

The Lord is good, a strong hold in the day of trouble; and he knoweth them that trust in him.
—*Nahum* 1:7

To my mom, Esther. You never doubted.

ONE

The knocking at the front door was unexpected.

Tanya Rivera dropped her purse and keys and a bag of takeout food onto the small, round kitchen table. She'd just gotten home a couple of minutes ago. Leaning toward her six-year-old nephew, Calvin, she gave him a light rub on the head. "Let me go see who that is." She immediately tried to smooth down the unruly lock of dark brown hair that was now sticking up near the back of his head. It refused to cooperate.

It had been a long day for the both of them. For the last four days, after school, he'd had to go sit in the office where

Tanya was employed as an accountant while she finished her work for the day. It would only be for eight more days, until his mom came home from a trip to Cozumel with a trio of friends, but it still appeared to be an overwhelming amount of disruption for the little boy.

Tanya glanced at the window. It was dark outside. Who would be coming by now? The unexpected knocking was repeated. Louder this time, sounding more insistent and impatient.

Whoever had come to her door demanding her attention had picked a bad time. She and Calvin were starving. She'd let the boy choose what they were having for dinner, but she'd told him he had to wait to eat until they got home. She'd thought that seemed like a parental thing to do.

Calvin sighed wearily.

Seeing the downcast expression on his little face, she reached into the bag and pulled out a container of onion rings. "Go ahead and take one," she said, setting the container on the table and giving him a kiss on his cheek. "I'll see who's at the door, and then we'll sit down together and eat our cheeseburgers."

He reached for an onion ring, and she turned and headed out of the kitchen, down the short section of hallway and toward the front door.

The doorbell rang.

"Coming!" she called out.

Narrow windows covered with a gauzy strip of fabric framed the door. Normally, Tanya would be able to see the outline of someone standing out there, even if she couldn't see enough detail to specifically identify them. But right now, she couldn't see a thing. The porch light was off. That was odd, because it had been on when she and Calvin got home a few minutes ago. The bulb must have burned out. Well, even the long-lasting ones didn't work forever.

"Who is it?" she called out as she reached for the door handle, realizing she should have checked her phone to see if someone she knew had texted to tell her they were stopping by. Too late. Her phone was tucked in her purse. She wasn't going back to the kitchen to get it.

"Pizza delivery," a male voice called out from the other side of the door.

Pizza? Must be for her neighbors a half mile down the road. Her house was on a winding, crumbly stretch of asphalt at the edge of town. Even with a map app, it could be confusing trying to find a specific house out here. Especially if you were a food-delivery person in a hurry.

Tanya unlatched the lock and opened the door.

The man standing on her front porch with a pizza box looked like he was maybe in his late twenties. Dark-haired, tall and skinny, he shifted his weight from foot to foot, and his gaze darted nervously around, never quite making eye contact with her.

"Hi." Tanya made herself smile. "You have the wrong address. I didn't order pizza."

"You sure? Maybe somebody else in the house ordered it. We run into that a lot." He moved up closer to the threshold, suddenly appearing focused on looking past her into the living room.

Tanya instinctively moved back. This guy was pushy, and she didn't much care for that. "Yeah, I'm sure. The Connells are the next house on this side of the street. They've got three teenagers. Maybe one of them ordered it."

The last few words came out of her mouth slowly as her mind began to process what she was seeing. Or more accurately, what she was *not* seeing. She had two exterior lights on the side of the garage visible from the front door. Both had been on when she'd arrived home. Neither one was burning now. And she knew for a fact that they were not on the same electrical circuit as her porch light, so it wasn't like something had happened to make all the outside lights go out at the same time.

Since the lights were on inside the house, she could see the top of the pizza box. She recognized the name of the pizza place it came from. It was an inexpensive national chain. They usually had illuminated signs attached to the tops of their delivery vehicles. She glanced toward her driveway and could just barely make out the outline of a pickup truck. It didn't have a sign. The headlights weren't on, and the engine wasn't running. Normally, delivery people left the engine idling.

A flicker of awareness came to life in the center of her stomach. *Something's wrong.* Images popped into her mind from news stories she'd seen about home invasions. Images of people tied up inside their own homes while they were terrorized and robbed.

Get a grip. There was no reason for anyone to invade and rob her nondescript little house. She was overreacting.

Except the guy wasn't wearing a pizza company hat or jacket like the drivers normally did. Just regular clothes, a coat with the hood pulled up over his head, and gloves.

While the suspicious thoughts wormed their way to the surface of her mind, the delivery guy's weight-shifting moves became even more agitated.

"Shouldn't you call your manager and get this delivery issue straightened out?" she said, and then immediately wondered why she'd told this guy how to do his job, but she was a problem solver by nature. It was part of why she became an accountant. She liked to get things in order and make sense of them.

The guy's phone chimed, and he pulled

it out of his pocket to glance at the screen. Tanya moved to close the door, but pizza guy stomped a muddy boot over the threshold to stop her.

"Back off!" Tanya snapped. She tried shoving the door closed, but his foot didn't budge.

Pizza guy looked up from his phone screen and settled his gaze on her. Tanya didn't like what she saw there. He had a hyperintense focus that did not belong on the face of someone just delivering pizza, and then he added the sudden flicker of a predatory smile. "Are you Tanya Rivera?" he asked. Without waiting for an answer, he threw down the pizza box and lunged at her.

Tanya tried again to slam the door shut, but it was too late. He already had half his body weight shoved forward with his foot and shoulder wedging the door. He gave the door a strong shove and forced it farther open. Shocked, Tanya jumped back, nearly stumbling over her own feet.

Calvin! Her heart thundered in her chest. What should she do? Yell out to Calvin to warn him? Shout for the little boy to hide? Yell at him to grab her phone from her purse and run out the back door? Could he even handle any of that?

Lord, help!

"What do you want?" she shouted as she quickly backed up and hit the light switch, plunging the living room into shadows. It wasn't completely dark because there were other lights on in the house, but maybe it would slow him down if he came after her. Maybe it would cause him to trip over something if he couldn't see the room clearly.

The man turned his head from side to side, as if he was looking for something. Or someone. Tanya reached for a heavy glass lamp on an end table, yanked the cord from the wall and held the lamp by her side, ready to swing it at the man. What else could she do? Run? The only other way out of the house was through the kitchen. If she ran for the back door, she'd lead this creep straight to Calvin. There's no way she would do that.

"My husband will be out here any minute," she lied. She didn't have a husband. "And he's got a gun." She didn't really have a gun in the house.

Pizza guy turned to her. She couldn't see his face clearly due to the shadows, but she could feel him staring at her. After initially forcing his way in, he hadn't chased her any farther. He didn't seem to be in a big hurry to grab her. Really, he didn't act at all like the impulsive criminal she'd presumed him to be when he'd lunged at her. He seemed to be taking in the situation, acting cold and calculated, like he had a *plan*.

"You don't have a husband, Tanya," he said. "You live alone."

This was the second time he'd used her name. He hadn't just randomly selected her house. The thought gave her chills.

"What do you want?" she demanded again. "I don't have any valuable jewelry. I don't keep much cash on hand, but I'll give you my purse and you can take the money, the credit cards, whatever that's in it, and go." He could have it all. The only thing she cared about right now was keeping Calvin safe.

What if this jerk followed her into the kitchen while she got her purse? Was it too much to hope that Calvin had heard the altercation at the front door and had hidden somewhere in the house?

She heard a rattling sound from the direction of the kitchen. Like maybe Calvin was trying to unlock the door to the backyard. She swallowed thickly, trying not to choke on the fear rising up. *Focus.* She had to stay rational in the middle of this bizarre and frightening situation, but her anxiety grew as she considered what might happen if this creep saw Calvin.

Pizza guy turned his face in the direction of the kitchen and the rattling sound.

"You haven't told me what you want," Tanya said loudly, desperate to turn the man's attention back to her.

"Ultimately, we want information from your sister, Dawn," he said, facing her again. "But right now, we're here to take the boy."

We? There was more than one stranger here? And they wanted Calvin?

The sudden explosive noise of breaking glass yanked her attention back to whatever was happening in the kitchen, and she heard the wood-splitting sound of the back door being forced open.

"Calvin!" Tanya flung the lamp at pizza guy and darted toward the kitchen, desperate to grab her nephew and get him out of the house and away from danger.

She was halfway down the hall to the

kitchen when pizza guy leaped on her, knocking her to the ground and grabbing hold of her ankles.

"There's no point in running," he growled.

She twisted an ankle free from his grip and kicked his face. He cursed at her, and she took advantage of his momentary surprise and was able to break free. She pushed herself to her feet and sprinted into the kitchen, shoving through the swinging door and coming up short.

Calvin stood by the table, eyes wide with fear, a half-eaten onion ring clutched in his fist. A stranger stood beside him, hand gripping the boy's small shoulder, holding him close.

"Leave him alone!" Tanya shouted, but she didn't dare move to grab her nephew, even though she desperately wanted to. The man holding Calvin was pointing a gun at her.

No! No, no, no! This could not be happening. *Lord, please!*

Pizza guy walked through the swinging door behind Tanya, red marks and scratches on his face from where she'd kicked him. He shoved her aside and moved toward his partner, a heavyset and balding man who appeared to be in his midforties.

Pizza guy's steps made crunching sounds as he walked over the broken glass scattered across the floor toward his accomplice. The back door had obviously been busted open and then shut, but the latch no longer closed tightly. Wind from the increasingly unsettled weather rattled the door and blew into the kitchen through the holes in the glass.

"Young Calvin here is going to accompany us on a trip," bald guy said. "He'll have fun, and it might encourage his mother to meet with us for a chat. We'll be in touch later with directions on how she can do that."

Though it was hard to even take a

breath, Tanya somehow managed to swallow her panic. Desperate screams were not going to help Calvin. "Take me with you," she said. She couldn't imagine what they wanted from Dawn, and most especially, what they could want so desperately that they would attempt to kidnap Calvin.

Dawn's trip to Mexico was a diversion with the friends who were supposed to have been her bridesmaids. It was intended to help her forget about the bum who'd jilted her just three weeks short of their wedding date. Could something have happened in Mexico? Was she in some kind of trouble there?

"Dawn wouldn't want you to hurt me," Tanya added quickly. "We're close." That was mostly true. She and her older sister weren't exactly on the outs, but they'd always been different personality types, and Tanya had developed a faith that Dawn didn't seem to understand. Still, they got along well when they were together. The birth of Calvin, followed by the pressures of being a single mom when Dawn and Calvin's father had parted ways, had most definitely helped draw the sisters together.

"I could be more helpful to you than the boy," she continued. "I could reason with my sister, convince her to give you whatever you want or find the information you're looking for." Words poured out of her like water. Driven by fear, she frantically tried to think of reasons why they'd want to take her instead of Calvin.

She could tell by their lack of response that her pleas were going nowhere. The bald guy with the gun started pressing on Calvin's shoulder to get him to turn around to face the back door. Pizza guy now stood halfway between Tanya and the bald guy, as if to keep her from interfering when the man took Calvin away.

"I won't give you any trouble," Tanya burst out. Tears poured down her face, and sobs rose up like a fist in her throat. "It will be easier for you if you take me. I won't make a scene. I won't do anything to draw attention to myself. Calvin is just a little boy. He'll get upset. He might yell and scream and make things harder for you."

She began to shake. She was losing it. She looked around, desperate for something she could use as a weapon, something to stop them, but there was nothing within reach. The wooden block full of sharp knives was up on top of the fridge. She'd started keeping it there back when Calvin was a toddler and had started to get into everything. Her phone was in her purse, which was pushed toward the back of the table. It might as well be a mile away.

She turned to Calvin. His wide-eyed gaze had stayed on her the whole time. Clearly, he thought she could save him. The expression of hopeful trust in his eyes nearly killed her. The wind blowing through the broken windows kicked up the tuft of hair on his head, the one that never wanted to stay down. A sudden gust blew the back door open, and it banged against the edge of the counter. Both gunmen turned toward the sound.

Calvin still had his gaze locked on Tanya. "Run!" she yelled.

The boy twisted and ducked and broke free of the bald guy's grasp. Tanya launched herself at the bald guy, focused on grabbing his gun, terrified he'd shoot at Calvin as he darted out the door.

Pizza guy grabbed a handful of Tanya's hair and yanked her head back, effectively pulling her away from the gunman and throwing her to the floor.

"Get the boy!" the bald guy shouted.

As pizza guy sprinted past her and out the door, Tanya pushed herself up onto her knees and grabbed at the bald guy's gun again, afraid he would go hunting for her nephew. He backhanded her so hard that she fell, and the side of her face slammed against the linoleum floor. For a second, she lay there stunned and unable to move.

Oh, Lord, help Calvin! she prayed.

Ignoring the sensation of her head spinning, she got to her feet. She stumbled unsteadily to the doorway. It was pitch-black outside. Rain was falling. Calvin and the two gunmen were nowhere in sight.

Bounty hunter Danny Ryan had been tailing his mark for three-quarters of an hour. He'd spent the last fifteen minutes in his SUV parked on the street, watching a house, trying to figure out what was going on inside.

Victor Durbin was relatively new to town, and after three months of living in Range River, Idaho, he'd stolen a brand-new, very big, fully outfitted luxury sedan. Victor had been caught, charged and subsequently released on bail. He'd purchased a bail bond through Range River Bail Bonds, Danny's employer, which also happened to be the Ryan family business.

Victor hadn't shown up for his court appearance this morning, his first mistake of the day. His second mistake had been boldly moseying into a pizza shop where he'd been spotted by one of Danny's informants.

Danny had caught up with Victor just as he and some guy left the restaurant with a pizza and drove away in a pickup truck. Danny wasn't a cop, so he wasn't authorized to make a traffic stop. Instead, he figured he'd follow them until they got to wherever they planned to eat their dinner, and then he'd arrest Victor and earn his recovery fee. The guy had some prior arrests, but nothing violent. The sedan he'd stolen had been unoccupied, so it wasn't like he'd pulled a gun on somebody. It should be a garden-variety collar.

The two men had headed toward the curving narrow roads that led up into the hills on the southern side of town. Danny had held back as he followed them, not wanting to risk them seeing him and speeding off. They'd passed through a stretch of forest until they reached the edge of a residential area with widely spaced houses. Figuring they were headed to a house around here, Danny had slowed down and dropped back even farther.

When he'd approached a house, and the exterior lights were suddenly extinguished, that caught his attention. Maybe it was a sign that Victor was there and he was trying to hide. Sure enough, as Danny slowly cruised by, he saw the truck he'd been following parked in the house's driveway. In the shadows, he could barely see one man standing at the front door. He was the same general size and shape as Victor.

Danny had driven by, turned around

and parked down the street to watch the house. If this had been Victor's home, Danny would have called one or two other bounty hunters, and they could forcefully insist on gaining entry to the residence. They were expressly given the right to do that in the bail-bond contract. But he couldn't do that in this situation, since he had no record of this being Victor's residence, so he sat, watched and waited.

Waiting was not Danny's strong suit.

Unfortunately, he didn't have his night-vision goggles with him. He saw Victor stay on the porch for a while and then kind of lurched inside. That was odd. And where was his friend?

Already tired of waiting, Danny got out of his SUV to have a look around. He quickly saw that the front door of the house had been left open. That was strange, since it was cold and windy, and anybody inside the house must have noticed the door was open by now.

The house had an attached garage, a few outbuildings and some trees, but no fencing. The open front door could be some kind of trap. Maybe the fugitive knew he was being followed. Danny had been in the office when Victor purchased his bond. He would recognize Danny as a bounty hunter. Perhaps he'd seen Danny and fled.

Danny decided to move around the garage and head toward the back of the house. He just wanted to get a quick look so he could figure out what he was dealing with and come up with a plan to capture his fugitive.

He'd barely cleared the corner of the garage when he heard a male voice coming from a cluster of trees several yards away. "Where *is* he?"

"Can't be far," a second voice that sounded like Victor's responded.

Where is who? Had they lost their dog? If so, this could be the perfect opportunity to grab Victor while he was distracted.

The back door of the house was open. What was it with these people's inability to close doors? Danny glanced over at the light spilling from the house, trying to gauge how he could stay hidden as he made his way over to grab Victor. His gaze swept over the glitter of smashed glass near the threshold. He realized the window in the door was broken.

"I'm not waiting!" a woman shouted, her voice choked with anguish. She was inside the house, in the kitchen, from what he could see. *"No!"* she shouted again.

Danny took a quick peek and saw the back of a woman with a phone to her ear.

"What if they find my nephew and start to leave with him?" she said into the phone. "I have to stop them. Tell the cops when they get here that I'll be outside doing whatever I can to protect Calvin. And that they need to be looking for the two men I already described to you."

A sharp blade of worry slashed through the pit of Danny's stomach. Had Victor and his friend done something to this woman's nephew? Had they hurt a *child*?

Danny stepped up to the threshold. The woman spun in his direction, dropped her phone, picked up a chair from a small dinette set and started swinging it at his head. He brought up his arms to block the blows.

"It's okay, I'm not going to hurt you," he said between hits. "I'm not one of the bad guys. I want to help."

Her eyes appeared glazed with fear, and if anything, his words seemed to make her determined to hit him even harder.

He didn't want to scare her, but they didn't have time to waste. The next time she swung, he grabbed the chair, twisted it and yanked it out of her hands.

She snatched a glass coffeepot from the counter and raised it, apparently planning to fling it at him.

Danny held up his hands. "I'm a bounty

hunter. I am pursuing one of those men. How do you know Victor Durbin?"

"Who?" The wildness in her eyes appeared to subside a little.

"I heard you on the phone," he said. "Sounds like a boy is missing, and Victor and his friend are after him for some reason. I just want to help."

She lowered the coffeepot slightly.

"You must have been talking to an emergency operator," Danny continued. It was hard to keep the impatience out of his voice. They were wasting time. The men might have already found the boy and taken off with him. "You can trust me. Look, I'm staying right here even though I heard you on the phone and I know the police are on the way. A lot of the cops in town know me. They'll vouch for me when they get here. In the meantime, I don't want to just stand here. How old is the boy they're looking for?"

"Six," she said, impatiently wiping tears from her eyes.

"Have you already looked for him?"

"No. I told him to run, and he ran. I'm afraid if I go to the places where I think he might hide, that will help these criminal jerks find him." More tears fell from her eyes. "Maybe I did the wrong thing."

"Where do you think he might have hidden?"

Her expression turned cagey, and she didn't answer.

"Okay, you stay here in case your nephew comes back," Danny said. "I'll go take care of Victor and his friend." He'd take care of them, all right. Terrorizing this woman and a little boy? He felt his face flush with anger. "It's probably better if your nephew stays where he's hiding until the cops get here."

"There he is!" The sound of Victor's shout carried into the house. It was immediately followed by the loud bang of

something heavy being slammed aside in one of the outside storage buildings.

The boy screamed.

Danny took off running out of the kitchen, across the expanse of lawn, headed in the direction of the terrified child. Wind whipped the tree branches in front of him, and the smattering of rain slickened the grass, undermining his traction. When he got to the storage shed, where he thought the scream had come from, it was empty. He spun around, frantically looking for the men and the boy. He didn't see them but reasoned they must be heading for their truck parked in the driveway. He took off running again.

He raced around the corner of the house to the truck. They weren't there. How could that be? They had to know the woman would have called the police. They must know they needed to make a fast getaway.

A second vehicle.

If they'd planned this abduction ahead

of time, they might have left a getaway vehicle parked nearby earlier in the day. Victor had the skills to steal whatever kind of ride they needed.

Danny tried to peer into the surrounding darkness. Which way would they have gone? *Take a breath and think.* It was almost as if he could hear his older brother's voice in his head. Danny tended to be the action guy. He'd been that way from the time he was a kid. But he'd learned that sometimes it was better if he made himself slow down just a little.

The road. Danny looked up and down the street. There were houses to the south, which meant potential witnesses if the bad guys hid a getaway car there. There was a stretch of forest to the north. Parking a car alongside the road over there would be less noticeable, which made it a more likely location.

He ran toward the stretch of forest, rounded a curve and saw them. Victor was trying to walk quickly down the small hill toward the street while holding a squirming little boy. His accomplice was farther ahead, inside a sedan and starting the engine.

Danny yelled out to his fugitive. "Victor! Let that boy go!"

The car thief—and now kidnapper—snapped his head around and took several stumbling steps before righting himself. His accomplice gunned the engine and drove up closer to the bottom of the hill.

Danny kept moving, closing the distance between them. He had a gun, but he wasn't going to use it when there was a child in the line of fire. He also had pepper spray. He wasn't thrilled at the thought of using that near a child, either, but it would be better than letting the boy get kidnapped.

Police sirens wailed in the distance. Close, but not close enough.

Danny heard rapid footsteps behind

him. He turned and saw the woman from the kitchen running toward him. She was carrying a baseball bat. She ran past Danny, making a beeline toward the getaway car.

Gunshots exploded out of the car's rear window, the bullets flying in the woman's direction. She ducked, but she didn't stop running. Danny caught up with her, trying to figure out if he should tackle her to stop her.

Up ahead, the boy screamed and kicked at Victor. They were nearly to the getaway car.

"No!" the woman screamed as she closed the gap between them, raw fury in her voice.

Victor turned to look in her direction, and his steps fumbled again. He dropped the crying, flailing boy. He bent to pick up Calvin, but the smart little guy rolled away.

Red and blue lights flickered through

the pine trees. The police were almost there. Victor turned toward the cop cars and then turned toward the boy, who was already on his feet and running toward the woman. For a split second, he appeared indecisive. Finally, he turned and sprinted to the getaway car, threw himself into the passenger seat, and the vehicle sped off.

The woman dropped to her knees and wrapped her arms around the boy.

Relief washed over Danny, but it was a measured, limited feeling of relief.

Anybody who was willing to put that much planning and effort into kidnapping a little boy was likely to try it again.

TWO

Danny flagged down the first of the arriving cops. The Range River Police Department patrol car pulled over to the side of the road, and Officer Jeremy Billings quickly exited the car. Danny had worked with him numerous times over the years.

"Is that the child who was reported missing?" Billings asked, gesturing toward the boy, who was still being hugged tightly by his relieved aunt.

Danny nodded. "Yes. That's Calvin." The bounty hunter quickly explained what had happened, including Victor's name and last known address and a physical description of the second assailant. "The kidnappers fled north just before you got here, so you must have seen their car drive past you." He told the officer what he could about the getaway car, though he hadn't been able to see it very well in the dark. "The light that should have illuminated the rear license plate was out. Probably intentionally disabled. So I didn't get the plate number."

Billings was already on his collar mic, calling in the car's description.

"The criminals arrived in a different vehicle and left it here. It's still in the driveway," Danny said as an officer strode over from the second patrol car. "It's a pickup truck. Victor Durbin is a car thief, so it's probably stolen."

"Go see if there's a plate on it and call it in if there is one," Billings said to the second officer, who nodded and then turned and headed toward the driveway.

"Why aren't you chasing them?" the woman, still holding the boy, called out as she hurried in their direction.

Danny turned his gaze on her, and for the first time, he felt the stirrings of recognition. Did he know her from somewhere? He pushed the thought aside for the moment and focused his attention on Calvin. "Are you okay?" he asked.

The little boy turned his face into the base of his aunt's neck and hugged her tighter.

"Physically, he's fine," the woman said, shifting her nephew's weight on her hip. "Just a few scratches. But emotionally, well, that was obviously a lot for him to go through." She blew out a puff of air to get her blond hair off her face before turning to the patrol officer. "So why isn't anybody going after them?" she asked impatiently.

"Ma'am, we have other units already working on this call," Billings said. "They've just been updated with a description of the suspects' car, and they are searching for it as we speak. An alert will go citywide and other patrol cars will be looking for them, as well."

Danny watched the anguish and frustration on the woman's face ease a little. He still didn't know where he recognized her from, and he was just about to ask her name when headlights flickered through the trees and an unmarked police sedan pulled up, its rear-window bank of emergency lights flashing. The car parked at the side of the road alongside the patrol cars. A woman with dark auburn hair pulled back in a tight bun and wearing a gray suit exited the car and walked toward them.

"Detective Romanov," Billings said quietly.

"Yep," Danny responded with a slight nod.

Billings walked over to intercept her, and after exchanging a few words, he headed toward the front of the house.

As the detective approached, she made

eye contact with Danny. As usual, she didn't look happy to see him. She and her husband, who worked for the district attorney's office, had moved to Range River from Los Angeles a little over a year ago. For some reason, she was never particularly enthusiastic to see one of the Range River bounty hunters at a crime scene.

"Tanya Rivera?" the detective asked as she approached.

Still holding the boy on her hip, the woman nodded. "Yes."

"Tanya Rivera?" Danny said aloud before he could stop himself. Now he realized why she looked familiar. He knew her from high school. The last time he'd seen her was at least twelve years ago. Back then she'd been a quiet girl who walked around with her nose in a book and helped out in the Eagle Rapids High School library. Danny had been a restless star football player who only stepped foot in the library if a class assignment required him to. Or when he was sent there to serve an hour's detention after school because his impulsive nature had gotten him into trouble. Again.

"I'm Danny Ryan," he said when she didn't immediately respond. "You and I went to school together."

She fixed her gaze on him for a moment, head tilted slightly, and then raised her eyebrows. "I remember you."

She didn't sound especially thrilled to see him again. Danny couldn't immediately think of a reason why that might be, but that didn't mean there wasn't one.

"Maybe the two of you can catch up on old times later," Detective Romanov said tightly to Danny. Then to Tanya, she said in a friendlier voice, "It's chilly out here. How about we go inside your house and you tell me what happened?"

The three of them began walking. Tanya had just started recounting the kidnapping attempt when Detective Romanov abruptly stopped walking and gave Danny a pointed look. "We don't need a bounty hunter right now."

"I think maybe you do," Danny responded politely but just as pointedly. "I tracked Victor Durbin here. Ultimately, I found him through an informant, but I did spend the late morning and early afternoon searching for him, talking to a couple of his associates, learning where he likes to hang out and what he likes to do in his spare time. Since you're going to be searching for him, don't you want to find out what I know?"

"Yes," Tanya said before the detective could answer. "Yes, we absolutely do."

Romanov sighed deeply, nodded, then turned around and resumed walking toward the house.

Tanya, still carrying Calvin, walked alongside her, and Danny followed. He wasn't trying to be a smart aleck. It wasn't his intention to get in the way of a police investigation or step on anyone's toes. He knew he wasn't a cop, but he was licensed to apprehend anyone who forfeited a bail bond. It was his job to track down anyone who violated a bail bond underwritten by Range River Bail Bonds. That included Victor. And after witnessing what had happened to Tanya and her nephew, he was even more determined to find Victor. Unless the cops found him first. And while Danny was at it, he wanted to track down Victor's criminal partner, too.

They entered the house and were just getting settled in the living room when a pair of crime-scene techs showed up. Danny heard one of them on a phone arranging to have the pickup truck in the driveway towed to the police department garage, where they could inspect it more thoroughly. He watched the techs bag the pizza box Victor had tossed when he forced his way into the house and then focus on lifting prints near the front and back doors to establish that Victor Durbin had been in the house. The prints would help in the case against Victor and would help them get a lead on identifying his accomplice.

Calvin relaxed enough to release his grip on his aunt and sit beside her on the sofa, though he didn't move very far away. Officer Billings walked in through the front door. At the detective's direction, he turned on the TV and started talking with the boy, distracting him so that Tanya and the detective could speak more candidly.

In response to Detective Romanov's promptings, Tanya began recounting step-by-step what had happened. Her voice sounded oddly flat and unemotional, and Danny figured she was still in shock. When she reached the point where Victor had asked about Calvin by name and mentioned Tanya's sister, her eyes grew wide. "Dawn! I need to call her and make sure she's okay."

She grabbed her phone and tapped the screen. "Seriously?" she called out a few seconds later to no one in particular. She ended the call and then tapped the screen to try again. "I'm getting a recording telling me the call can't go through," she said with the phone to her ear, this time directing her comments to the detective. "Dawn's in Mexico. I saw something on the news about a hurricane forming in the Caribbean, but Dawn said it wasn't projected to move in the direction of the resort where she's staying."

Danny reached for his own phone and did a quick online news search.

"This attempt isn't going through, either," Tanya muttered, disconnecting.

"Is Dawn in the Yucatán Peninsula?" Danny asked.

"Yes."

"The hurricane unexpectedly shifted westward before making landfall about three hours ago. It was a direct hit on Cancún."

Tanya burst into tears.

"The police department can go through governmental channels and request that local law enforcement check on your sister," Detective Romanov said. After getting the pertinent information from Tanya, she quickly sent a text and then set aside her phone. "Tanya, I know you're worried, and I don't blame you. But right now, I need you to finish telling me everything that happened."

Tanya glanced at her nephew, who'd moved slightly away from her to quietly watch TV with Officer Billings. She took a deep breath, faced the detective and resumed her description of the events, including Danny's arrival on the scene. She turned in his direction as she talked about him, and he found himself thinking about the courage she'd demonstrated in such a horrible and unexpected situation. As far as he knew, she didn't have the training he had to deal with violent, deranged people. She hadn't had any weapons at hand, but she'd made good use of a chair, a coffee-pot and a baseball bat.

Tanya Rivera, library girl, had the heart of a lioness. Who knew?

"Is your sister involved in anything illegal?" Detective Romanov asked quietly with a glance toward Calvin to make sure he wasn't listening.

Tanya's eyebrows shot up toward her hairline, and she vehemently shook her head. "No. Absolutely not."

"Drugs?" the detective continued. "Maybe a boyfriend involved with drugs? Sadly, decent people sometimes end up making bad decisions for someone they love. Or someone they *think* they love."

Danny felt a small, sharp knot in the pit of his stomach. It seemed Dawn was involved in something that had put little Calvin in danger. The detective was right, people did sometimes do awful things for the sake of what they believed was love. He'd certainly seen his share of it. Love, *romantic* love, was a minefield as far as he was concerned.

"No," Tanya repeated more forcefully. "Dawn experimented with drugs when she was younger, but she doesn't use them anymore, and right now, she doesn't have a boyfriend. She was engaged, but the jerk broke it off three weeks before the ceremony. That's why she's in Mexico. Everything was already paid for. He told her to get refunds on whatever she could and do whatever she wanted with the money. So she did just that and paid for three of her girlfriends to join her on a vacation in Mexico. I volunteered to stay here and look after Calvin."

"This former fiancé, do you think he holds some kind of grudge against her?" Romanov asked.

Tanya shook her head. "He told her he

felt they'd drifted apart and that it would be a mistake to go through with the wedding. He thought they should go their separate ways."

"What's his name?" the detective asked.

"Elliott Bridger."

"Is he Calvin's father?"

"No. His father's name is Joe Flynn."

"Any problems between your sister and Mr. Flynn?"

"No."

"Does she owe anyone money?"

Tanya shrugged. "That's not something we've talked about. She has a mortgage, like I do. A car loan. Maybe some credit card debt. The usual stuff."

The detective nodded and then turned to Danny. "All right, bounty hunter, now's your time to shine. Tell me what you know about Victor Durbin that could help us find him."

Information from talking to actual human beings was what he had. Stuff beyond the impersonal data you could read off a computer screen. "I know he's behind on his rent, and his landlord and neighbors haven't seen him for over a week. One neighbor saw him selling his car outside his home. The neighbor walked over and chatted with him. Victor told him he hadn't been able to find work, at least not work that he wanted to do, and that he'd finally realized the odds of him ever having a good life were stacked against him. That playing by the rules doesn't pay off."

"Going from stealing unoccupied cars to home invasion and attempted kidnapping *is* quite an escalation in violence," Romanov said. "It does sound like Victor has settled on making crime his career."

"Knowing a fugitive's mind-set helps to find him," Danny continued, now directing his comments to Tanya. "And it gives you a good idea of how to deal with him when you do find him." He turned back to

Romanov. "Victor Durbin's gone over the edge, and he's working with an equally violent partner. We know that now. Beyond that, I've got to admit that it wasn't brilliant tracking skills that got me on his trail tonight. I actually found him because I sent out his photo to my informants, and one of them saw him and called me."

The detective gave a slight nod. "I know you're going to be out looking for Victor Durbin to earn your bounty recovery fee, but right now, he's part of an active investigation, so I want you to keep us informed about what you learn as you go about your business."

"Of course," Danny said. "And it would be helpful to me if you would do the same."

Romanov lifted an auburn eyebrow.

"You have your methods of searching for people that aren't available to me," Danny continued. "But there are also things I can do that you can't. Not legally.

And there are people who won't talk to cops but will talk to a bounty hunter." He took a deep breath and blew it out. "At the end of the day, we both want the same thing."

This wasn't the first time he'd given her a version of this speech, but maybe he and his bounty-hunting team had built up enough credibility with her to earn some respect by now. He understood her perspective. She was likely concerned that bounty hunters would overstep their legal limits when apprehending someone and possibly cause a future criminal conviction to be overturned on a technicality. That was the last thing he and his team wanted to do. So they were careful about following the rules. Mostly.

"Keep me informed," Romanov finally said. "And when I have information I can share with you without jeopardizing the case, I'll do it."

"Deal," Danny said. It looked like he

was finally making progress with the hard-nosed detective.

Romanov turned to Tanya. "I haven't seen video cameras or any other sign of a home security system in the house. You might want to do something about that."

Danny made a mental note to help Tanya get a security system installed.

The crime-scene techs finished their tasks, packed up and left, and Tanya stood and took the couple of steps over to talk to Calvin. The boy reached out to wrap an arm around his aunt. He didn't seem as frightened as he'd appeared earlier. Officer Billings got to his feet, patted the boy on the knee and said goodbye.

Detective Romanov pulled out a business card and handed it to Tanya. "I have your contact information, so as soon as we learn anything about your sister from the Mexican authorities, we'll let you know. The officers making their routine patrols tonight will keep this area, and your house in particular, well covered. In the meantime, if you think of anything you want to tell me, give me a call. You might want to stay somewhere else until we find the assailants. Or at least until you can make repairs to your back door and get a good security system installed."

Shortly after that, the detective and the remaining patrol officer left.

The wind was still blowing outside, and Danny could hear the damaged back door rattling from where they were in the living room. He walked into the kitchen and saw that someone had propped the kitchen table against the door to keep it closed since the latch was broken. And, of course, the window in the door had been shattered.

Tanya and Calvin walked in behind him.

"I'd be happy to fix this for you," he said to Tanya.

She sighed heavily, and her eyes glistened with tears. Danny had a pretty good idea of what she was going through. The stunned shock and disbelief about what had happened to her earlier was wearing off. Reality was settling in, and it was probably hitting her with a pretty hard punch.

"Thank you, I would appreciate it." Her voice broke on the final word, and tears began to roll down her cheeks.

Tanya and Calvin stood in the cold, breezy kitchen, holding on to one another, and Danny's heart broke just a little. This case wasn't about him recovering a bounty fee anymore. It was about doing everything he could for a woman who needed his help. And it was about protecting a vulnerable little boy. There was no telling what the two of them would be going up against moving forward. He couldn't leave them to fight their battles alone.

Tanya wiped away her tears and did her best to pull herself together. She didn't want to have a complete breakdown in front of Calvin and scare him. The poor kid had already been through enough.

She shifted her gaze to Danny Ryan, who was standing in front of her on his phone talking to somebody who was apparently going to bring over supplies to help repair her door and the window.

Danny Ryan. The object of a lot of teen girls' dreams at Eagle Rapids High School back in the day was in her kitchen. She almost laughed. Who would have ever thought that would happen?

He looked different than he had the last time she'd seen him. He was more muscular and filled out, and maybe his demeanor had toned down a bit. He seemed a little more focused and a lot less hyper.

He'd flirted with her a few times back when they were in high school. The school had had a dedicated library filled with books as well as a media room, and when he'd been in the library, he'd talked to her instead of doing whatever assignment he'd been sent there to do. Or he'd talked to her when he'd been sent there because he was in trouble and was supposed to sit silently.

She'd known at the time the attention he paid her was nothing personal. He'd been a football player and a class clown. He'd been friendly to all the girls, and yeah, maybe she'd had just a little bit of a crush on him back then.

Right now, she realized he'd just said something and was waiting for her to answer. "I beg your pardon?" she said.

"I asked you if there is somewhere you want me to take you and Calvin. Maybe a place you'd like to stay tonight other than here. Like with a family member."

"You think the thugs will come back," she said dully as cold, hard fear settled in the pit of her stomach. She quickly looked around for Calvin and was relieved to see he was focused on retrieving an action figure toy he'd left on the counter earlier this morning and wasn't listening to their conversation.

As she watched him, the reality of their situation threatened to bury her under yet another layer of dread. Victor Durbin and his criminal partner might possibly evade the cops tonight. And then they might come back and try to grab Calvin again.

"My parents don't live in town anymore," she said, turning back to Danny while thinking out loud. Her parents had parted ways, and her dad had left town when Tanya and Dawn were little. A year after Tanya graduated from high school, her mom and her mom's new husband had moved to Arizona to escape north Idaho's harsh winters.

Of course she had friends that she and Calvin could stay with, but she wanted to go someplace where Calvin would feel comfortable. "I'll call my aunt."

Aunt Winnie and Uncle Matt lived in an old Victorian house surrounded by apple trees and pine forest. The inside of the house always smelled like apple pie, which was in itself a comfort. Calvin liked to visit there. Tanya grabbed her phone and tapped the screen. After several rings the call went to voice mail. "Hey, Aunt Winnie," she said into the phone. "Would you please call me as soon as you get this? It's very important. Thanks."

Danny watched and listened as she left the message. She meant to sound calm, but she could hear the shakiness in her own voice. *Someone tried to kidnap Calvin, and they nearly got away with it.* The fearful reality of what had almost happened kept walloping her like a cold, hard wave. She took a deep breath and blew it out. The tremble in her voice had now migrated to her hands and the pit of her stomach. For Calvin's sake, she did her best to hold it together and blink back the tears forming yet again in the corners of her eyes.

She tried calling Uncle Matt but got his voice mail greeting as well. She left him the same message. There was no point in adding the details of what had happened tonight and sending them into a panic. After that, she tried to call her sister again, but just as before, the call wouldn't go through.

She felt very alone, despite Calvin and Danny being in the room with her. She had to remind herself she was never truly alone. Her faith had taught her that God would always be with her. She prayed a silent prayer. *Please, Lord, protect Calvin and Dawn. And me.*

A short time later, she heard a notification sound on Danny's phone. He glanced at the screen. "My sister and our friend, another bounty hunter, are here." He stood. "We'll get your door and window secured in no time."

Tanya followed him as he walked to the front door and opened it. A woman with reddish-blond hair and deep blue eyes like Danny's stood there holding a toolbox and a shopping bag from a hardware store. A dark-haired, brown-eyed man stood beside her holding a sheet of plywood.

"This is my sister, Hayley," Danny said as the woman stepped over the threshold. "And maybe you remember Wade Fast Horse. He went to school with us. He works for the family business, Range River Bail Bonds, along with my sister, my older brother and me."

"I'm sorry this happened to you," Hayley said. She looked maybe two or three years younger than Danny.

"Happy to help you any way we can," Wade added.

Tanya thought Wade looked a little familiar, but she wasn't sure. Maybe they'd had some classes together back in high school. "Thank you for your help," she said to both of them. She introduced them to Calvin, who immediately appeared fascinated by the big sheet of plywood Wade was carrying.

"Hey, little man, do you like to build things?" Wade asked.

Calvin wordlessly stared at him.

"Well, you can help me if you want to," Wade said as Danny led the new arrivals toward the kitchen, with Tanya and Calvin following.

Hayley and Wade started working on their repairs, making a bit of a racket. Calvin appeared determined to get in their way. The bounty hunters didn't seem to mind, though.

"It's possible that Victor and his accomplice personally want whatever information they think your sister has," Danny said, moving closer to Tanya and taking advantage of the noise from the repairs to talk to her candidly while her nephew was distracted. "But my gut tells me they were hired by somebody else to get the information. Do you have any theories on who that might be?"

Tanya shook her head. "I have absolutely no idea."

"Is there anything you can tell me that you didn't mention to the police?"

Hot anger flared through Tanya, and she felt her face turning red. "After everything I've been through tonight, you accuse me of withholding information from the police investigating the crime? *Really?*"

Danny calmly held up both hands in a placating gesture. "Look, people do all kinds of things for all kinds of reasons. I'm not a mind reader, so to do my job, I have to ask direct questions. If you want to get offended, that's your choice."

Tanya took a deep breath and blew it out. Danny Ryan might be somebody she'd known back in high school, but he wasn't here as her friend. He was a bounty hunter doing his job, and she needed to remember that. Anything he said or asked wasn't personal.

"I understand," she finally said. "Ask me whatever you need to."

"Good. What about Joe Flynn, Calvin's dad? Could this be related to a custody dispute?"

"Joe wouldn't do anything like this."

"That's not what I asked you."

Tanya bit back a sharp response and reminded herself again that the man was just trying to do his job.

"So *is* there an ongoing custody dispute?" Danny pressed.

"When Dawn found out she was going to have Calvin, Joe told her he wasn't interested in being a dad. Or staying with Dawn. They never married. Joe met his financial obligations, but that was it. And then, a couple of years ago, when Calvin was four, Joe wanted back into their lives. Dawn was hesitant at first, but she finally decided to slowly introduce Calvin to him. I don't think Calvin sees him as anything more than one of his mom's friends."

And now that she thought of it, maybe that was part of the problem with Elliott. Maybe that was why he'd backed out of the wedding. Maybe he thought Dawn and Joe were getting back together. Or perhaps he realized he didn't want to be a father figure to Calvin.

She shook her head, trying to clear her thoughts. "I just can't see Joe putting Calvin in danger. Victor's accomplice had a *gun*. Shots were fired. Calvin could have been hurt." *Or killed.* She looked over at her nephew, wanting the reassurance that he really was okay. One of the bounty hunters had apparently given him a silvery tape measure to hold, and he appeared fascinated by it.

A short time later, Hayley and Wade finished their repairs and said their goodbyes.

"We'll wait for you outside," Hayley said to Danny.

Wade and Calvin shared a fist bump as the bounty hunter walked out the front door.

Tanya felt a smile cross her lips. At this moment, at least, the little boy seemed to have recovered from his earlier trauma. But who knew what would happen when he tried to fall asleep later tonight?

"I'm going to call my aunt and uncle again," Tanya said to Danny. She hadn't heard back from either of them. As before, the calls went to voice mail.

"Have you and Calvin had dinner?" Danny asked.

Tanya gestured toward the bag of fast food lying on its side on the table and the cold onion rings scattered around it.

"Why don't you let me take you and Calvin out for something to eat? It might take your mind off things for a little while. Give you something to do besides sit and worry while you wait to hear back from your aunt and uncle."

The fact was she was going to be sitting and worrying about Calvin's safety and what was happening with her sister in Mexico no matter where she was tonight, even if she were sitting in a restaurant. But maybe going out to eat would give Calvin a feeling of normalcy. And Tanya wouldn't mind a little more time under the protection of bounty hunter Danny Ryan while she figured out how to keep Calvin safe from the threat of another attack, whether from Victor and his accomplice or someone else. Maybe someone who'd hired them. Right now it felt like anything was possible, and she had no idea how to prepare herself and Calvin for what could happen next.

THREE

Danny pulled his jacket closer together in front of his chest and flipped up the collar. The on-and-off drizzle had stopped for the moment, but the wind was still blowing. He walked across the front lawn of Tanya's house until he reached a point where he could see up and down the street and make certain the scene was secure. Working together, Tanya and Calvin got Calvin's jacket zipped up as they stood on the front porch, and then Tanya locked the front door.

The pickup truck the criminals had abandoned in the driveway had already been towed away by the police.

Hayley and Wade got out of the SUV

where they'd been waiting and walked over to Danny.

"What's the plan?" Hayley asked.

"Right now, I'm going to get them some dinner." Danny glanced at Tanya and Calvin as they headed toward him. "I plan to stick close to them until Tanya gets things lined up to stay with her aunt tonight."

"If they need a place to stay, Connor's got room. Connor's always got room," Hayley commented decisively.

Danny and Hayley had the same parents, and Connor was their older half brother. All three had the same father. After Connor's mom passed away, he'd inherited the run-down old Riverside Inn on the banks of the Range River. The inn wasn't very big, but it was a historic building, and it was handsome and cozy once Connor finished refurbishing it.

He didn't rent out any of the six bedrooms to the general public, but he was generous with letting family and friends stay there when they needed a place. Even though Danny and Hayley each had their own apartments, they nevertheless stayed at the inn on occasion.

Their father and Danny and Hayley's mother had died in a car crash when Connor had just turned twenty-one. Like their dad, Connor had been more than a little wild at the time, but he'd immediately petitioned for custody of his siblings so they wouldn't be put into foster care. Danny had been eleven at the time. Hayley was seven.

"No doubt, Connor has room at the inn," Danny said in response to his sister's comment. "But my first choice would be for them to stay somewhere that's familiar to them. I think that's especially important for Calvin."

"All right," Tanya called out, holding Calvin's hand as she stepped up to them. "I think we're ready to go."

"Does Mining Company Barbecue sound good to you?" Danny said.

Tanya nodded. "Sure."

"Hayley and I will follow you," Wade said to Danny. "We'll make sure you all get there safely and then head to the office to research where Victor Durbin might go to hide."

After they arrived at the restaurant and he could communicate with him more subtly, Danny would send Wade a text asking him to see what information he could uncover on Tanya's sister, on her former fiancé and on Calvin's father, Joe. Sometimes the closest, most trusted people in a person's life turned out to be the most dangerous, but talking about that possibility right now in front of Tanya seemed like it would be unnecessarily alarming to her.

"Why would somebody need to follow us to the restaurant?" Tanya asked Danny, her voice tense. "Why wouldn't we get there safely?"

"They'll just hang back and make sure no one is tailing us," Danny answered easily. "A little extra security at no extra charge." He winked at Tanya, hoping to lighten the mood by eliciting a laugh or at least a slight smile.

Instead, she frowned.

Of course, Hayley laughed. He knew his little sister wasn't laughing at his lame joke. She was laughing at *him*. Clearly, his attempt at turning on the charm was a swing and a miss.

With Tanya giving directions, Danny managed to get Calvin's booster seat out of her car and into his SUV. Once the three of them were settled in, Danny drove down along the winding road and into the town of Range River. In the distance, he could see lights reflecting off the waterway the town was named after.

Calvin was quiet during the ride, apparently engrossed in playing a video game on the tablet Tanya had handed him. Tanya was subdued, too. Nearly every time Danny glanced over at her, she was staring out the window.

He kept a close watch on their surroundings as he drove, though it was hard to see much of what was around them until they reached the lights in town.

"I'm going to try to call Dawn again," Tanya said as they pulled into the restaurant parking lot.

Her call didn't go through.

Danny looked toward the street in time to see Wade's SUV drive by. Shortly after, he received a text from his sister confirming they hadn't seen anyone tailing Danny's SUV. He replied with his request for them to expand their online research beyond Victor Durbin.

Danny continually scanned the area around them as they headed into the restaurant. He knew the hostess, and at his request, she seated the three of them in a booth in the back, away from doors and windows. He also knew the owner could be relied upon to keep a cool head if anyone tried to make trouble here. Suggesting this place for dinner hadn't been random.

Once they were settled, Tanya asked Calvin to pause his game and take off his headphones long enough to decide what he wanted to eat. Once that task was taken care of, she let him go back to playing.

"I don't normally set up my nephew with a game and then ignore him," Tanya said as she sat back and crossed her arms over her chest in a defensive posture. "But right now, I just want him to do whatever he needs to be calm."

"I'm not judging you," Danny responded after taking a sip of water from the glass their waitress had set in front of him. "You've been through a lot, and you're doing a good job of holding it together for his sake."

After a moment, she uncrossed her arms. "Thank you."

The waitress came back, took their orders and then left.

"So what have you been doing since high school?" Danny asked, figuring maybe she wanted to unwind a little and talk about something other than the attack.

"I haven't been doing anything as exciting as bounty hunting," she responded. "How'd you get started with that?"

If she didn't want to talk about herself, that was fine. Danny wouldn't push her.

"My family owns a bail bonds business, and we recover bail jumpers when we need to," he said. "My older brother, Connor, started it. He worked as a bounty hunter and then got licensed to sell bail bonds. I followed in his footsteps, and so did Hayley. Wade has been a friend since he and I were twelve, and he eventually got pulled into our orbit, too. We consider him family." He rubbed a finger along the side of his water glass. "I was a little out of control in high school. I went into the army after I graduated, and it was a good experience for me. I learned a few things that ended up helping me with bounty hunting."

"I remember how you were as a teenager." Tanya nodded, and a slight smile lifted one corner of her mouth.

Danny couldn't help smiling in return, though it was mostly out of embarrassment. He'd been a goofball back then. There was no denying it.

Her smile began to fade. "Why do bounty hunters chase after bad guys instead of the cops doing it? And why do bail bondsmen help criminals get released onto the streets in the first place?"

Reasonable questions. He'd heard them fairly often. "To begin with, our legal system presumes a person is innocent until proven guilty. If someone is arrested and there's no compelling evidence that they're a danger to society, a judge will set bail so they can move about freely, but with some restrictions, until they go to trial.

"If they can't afford the full amount of the bail, they can come to us to purchase a bail bond. They pay a fee plus put up collateral in case they disappear, so that if they forfeit their bail and we have to pay the full bond amount on their behalf, we can get our costs back. If they show up in court like they're supposed to, everything is fine.

"As far as the police are concerned, they do look for fugitives. But a lot of the time, they're stretched thin staying on top of current crime. As bounty hunters, we don't try to get in their way or solve crimes. We just try to capture the people who failed to honor the contract they signed with us agreeing to show up in court. Occasionally, they commit a new crime, and their bail is revoked. At that point, we need to find them immediately and bring them in."

"Sounds like a stressful way to earn a living."

Danny shrugged. "I was always on the hyper side as a kid. I'm still a little bit that way. For me, sitting at a desk all day is stressful."

"I'm an accountant," Tanya said. "I spend a lot of time in front of a computer, usually sitting. The biggest threat I face on a daily basis is the possibility of high blood pressure when I have to deal with an obnoxious client."

"An accountant." Danny nodded. "So you're probably an organized person who keeps up on details. I'd say you like to plan things before you do them."

"That's a pretty good job of profiling me. And yeah, you should see my collection of planners. I'm old-school. Paper binders and lots of various-colored pens.

Electronic calendars and reminders just aren't hands-on enough for me."

She laughed, seemingly at herself. A moment later, the smile faded, and she rubbed her hands over her arms as if she were cold. Danny was pretty sure her thoughts had drifted back to the attack earlier tonight.

"They almost got away with Calvin," she said quietly after a quick glance at her nephew to make sure his earphones were plugged in and he was still wrapped up in his game.

Red splotches appeared on her face, and she blinked rapidly as her eyes turned watery. "I don't even know if Dawn is okay. Maybe she got into some kind of trouble in Mexico before the hurricane struck. Maybe the storm knocked apart the resort where she's staying. Maybe she's buried under the rubble, desperate for help."

"That's a lot of maybes," Danny said gently. "Maybe she is in trouble. But maybe she's okay. Right now, the best thing we can do is take whatever life throws at us one step at a time and keep her in our prayers."

"Prayers, yes," Tanya said, sniffing loudly and nodding her head. "I've already been praying for her."

Danny met her gaze and held it. "I'll pray for her, too." He would pray for Tanya, and for Calvin and his mom, as well. At the same time, he would also do everything he could to hunt down the criminals who had terrorized Tanya and Calvin tonight and bring them to justice.

The waitress delivered their meal. Tanya made Calvin take off his headphones and pause his game while they ate. Danny found himself enjoying the boy's conversation, which mostly focused on the adventures of some story or game characters Danny had never heard of.

They were nearly at the end of their meal when Tanya got a call from her aunt.

She and her husband had been at a bowling tournament. Without going into detail about what had happened earlier in the evening, Tanya asked if she and Calvin could come over and spend the night. By her reaction, it was obvious that her aunt thought that was a great idea.

Danny signaled for the check and paid it. The meal had been to his benefit as well as theirs. As a bounty hunter, he spent a lot of time around rough people. Despite the horrible circumstances that had brought them together, this dinner with Tanya and her young nephew had made him feel a little bit better about people in general. It was a nice glimpse into what a warm, normal family was like.

As they walked out of the restaurant and back to his SUV, he again kept his gaze moving so that he was aware of all their surroundings. "I'll take you by your house to get your car, and then I'll follow you to your aunt and uncle's house," he said after they were safely inside the vehicle.

"Okay, thanks."

Once she and Calvin arrived safely at her aunt and uncle's house, he remained parked nearby for a while to make certain they hadn't been followed. While he was doing that, he texted Detective Romanov to let her know where Tanya and Calvin were staying so she could have patrol officers keep an eye on that location throughout the night.

The whole idea of someone ruthlessly trying to grab a young boy in order to extort information from his mother smacked of something big. It reeked of desperation that could end in Tanya and Calvin getting hurt. Or maybe even killed.

It felt to Tanya like her coworkers tiptoed around her at the office the following morning. She'd told them about what had happened to her and Calvin last night.

Her employer and mentor, Helen Camden, had immediately suggested that she take the day off. In fact, Helen had said she could take whatever time she needed away from work. But Tanya couldn't just leave. Helen had been kind and supportive since the day Tanya had first showed up at the small accounting firm to apply for a position as a data-entry clerk. Her mentor had helped her pursue a degree in accounting and fostered her dreams of opening her own accounting business someday.

Helen had been fighting a long battle with diabetes, and these days her eyesight was failing. At the very least, Tanya wanted to get several of her projects organized and ready for one of the other accountants to take over so that Helen wouldn't have to do it. As soon as she had things organized, she'd leave.

She glanced at the wall clock. It was just after eleven. Her plan was to be ready to leave by noon. Aunt Winnie had already called, apologizing for interrupting her at work but feeling compelled to tell her that Calvin kept asking about Tanya. He was worried the *mean men* had taken her.

Tanya's phone chirped. It was a text message from Danny, and she felt a little flutter of butterflies in her stomach, which was ridiculous. The reaction had to be the result of not getting enough sleep last night. She wasn't interested in Danny Ryan. She was just tired.

Are you at your office? the text read. Do you have a few minutes to talk?

Yes, still at the office, she replied. Will be free to talk in about twenty minutes.

See you then, he replied.

Last night, sitting in the restaurant, there might have been a moment or two when she'd felt a little pull of attraction toward him. But he was just a man doing his job. Last night hadn't been a date. Beyond that, she'd known him to be a fairly self-centered flirt for the four years they'd gone to school together.

True, they were both kids at that time and had done substantial growing up in the years since then. Danny *appeared* more solid, like he had more depth of character, but appearances could be deceiving. And people didn't change, not at their inner core, not really.

She'd watched her parents split apart and get back together close to a dozen different times when she was growing up. She'd overheard one or the other claim they'd changed, *really* changed, after a separation and insist things would get better going forward.

Neither of them ever changed, though, and things never got better. Her dad had continued to drink instead of dealing with his emotions. Her mom kept blaming everyone but herself when it came time to pay the consequences for her own foolish decisions.

Finally, her parents had split for good. *People don't change*, her mom had said over and over again for the first year or so after the breakup. And to Tanya, that appeared to be the truth.

Danny Ryan had likely been on his best behavior last night. Maybe it had only *appeared* like he had some depth of character. That was fine. The man was a bounty hunter who'd shown up when she'd needed help and then offered his support and compassion. She appreciated that. Truly. But that was where it was all going to end.

The unruly butterflies that fluttered in her stomach when she thought of him were just going to have to flutter away and bother some other chump. Not her.

She dived back into her work and had things nearly wrapped up when Danny arrived at the office. He looked handsome in jeans, a long-sleeved navy blue shirt and cowboy boots. He held a black cowboy hat in his hand as he stepped inside the building. His appearance did not help her intention to stay emotionally detached. Not one bit.

She ushered him into her office, where he sat in a visitor's chair as she dropped down into her office chair behind her desk.

"So, how are you and Calvin holding up?" he asked.

"I'm doing okay," Tanya said. And overall, she was. Once she'd realized she needed to turn her thoughts toward prayer when she started to worry, she'd done exactly that, and she'd begun to feel stronger and better equipped to take care of Calvin and herself.

"Have you gotten any word about your sister?"

Tanya nodded. "Detective Romanov called me early this morning. She heard back from the authorities in Mexico. A couple of police officers went to the resort where Dawn and her friends are staying to check on several Americans with worried relatives. The officers saw Dawn and her friends, and they said she's fine and that the structure of the resort buildings is safe and secure. Electrical lines are down in the area, and the cellular phone system is overwhelmed and still experiencing connectivity issues, but service is expected to be restored soon. Dawn will call me as soon as she can."

Danny nodded. "That's good news."

"Detective Romanov also told me she'll be putting together a collection of mug shots for me to look at, and maybe I'll be able to identify Victor Durbin's accomplice. She said they're still processing all the fingerprints that were lifted from my house and inside the stolen pickup truck the kidnappers left behind in my driveway."

"Well, we at Range River Bail Bonds are on the job, as well."

"And what exactly does that mean?"

"Hayley and Wade are out and about as we speak, trying to find people who know Victor and who might know where he likes to hang out or where he would hide if he were in trouble."

"Why would people who know him want to help you find him?"

"Cash. Cold, hard cash will motivate a lot of people to spill the goods on their supposed friends."

"That's sad."

Danny shrugged. "I still want to talk to Calvin's dad, Joe."

Tanya shook her head. "I don't think you'll find a problem there."

She hadn't called Joe to tell him about the attempted kidnapping of his son. As far as Tanya was concerned, it was up to Dawn to decide what and when she wanted to tell Joe.

"I want to talk to your sister's former fiancé, too."

"Yeah, well, I want to talk to Dawn." Tanya sat back in her chair. "I'm anxious to hear that she's okay, and then I want to find out if she got into some kind of trouble in Mexico. Maybe Victor and his accomplice were hired by someone down there."

"Well, please let me know what you learn as soon as you talk to her."

"I will." Tanya pulled open a desk drawer to grab her purse. "Right now, I need to get back to my aunt's house to see Calvin."

"I'll follow you and make sure you get there okay."

"Thanks, but I got here on my own this morning without any trouble."

"That might be because the bad guys didn't know where you were staying last night. It's likely they know where you work. That means there's a possibility they know where you are right now."

A chill passed over Tanya's skin.

"If I follow you back to your aunt's house, I'll be able to tell if anyone else is following you."

As a regular everyday person, she didn't think a whole lot about personal security. She just tried to use common sense. It was unnerving to consider how many ways she could put herself in danger and not even realize it.

"You make a good point," she said. "Thank you."

A few minutes later, she was in her car and headed toward her aunt and uncle's house in the foothills south of town. Danny didn't stay close behind her, but every now and then she caught a glimpse of his vehicle in her rearview mirror. She assumed he was being subtle so that if anyone were following her, he could take them by surprise and catch them.

After rising in elevation and passing through several curves in the road, she turned onto the drive to her aunt and uncle's home. She headed up the narrow private road through the evergreens, glancing in the mirror a couple of times and feeling irrationally disappointed when she didn't see Danny's SUV following behind her. He must have decided to keep to the public street.

The house came into view, and Tanya parked on the expanse of gravel beside it. She was getting out of the car when her phone rang. Relief swept over her when she looked at the screen. Dawn was finally calling her. "Are you all right?" Tanya said as soon as she tapped Answer.

"Of course!" The reception was a little crackly, but it was clearly Dawn on the other end of the call. Tanya could hear the laughter in her sister's voice. "I'm at a gorgeous resort that looks like a giant hacienda. The power was knocked out by the storm, and things were a little dicey for a short while, but the resort has emergency generators, and they were able to get the lights back on and the party restarted in no time."

Clearly, after enduring the stress of an abruptly canceled wedding, Dawn was determined to enjoy her vacation no matter what. But her exuberance must mean that nothing bad, other than the hurricane, had happened to her while she was in Mexico.

Unless this was all an act.

While Dawn chattered, seemingly without taking a breath, Tanya decided not to go into the house just yet. She needed to talk to her sister frankly, without having to worry if Calvin was nearby and listening. She began to walk aimlessly around the grounds at the front of the house and over to the edge of the forest. She planned to let her sister finish what she wanted to say before telling her about the kidnapping attempt. Then she'd press to see if Dawn was really telling the truth about her experience in Mexico.

"You need to come down here to the

Yucatán as soon as you have vacation time," Dawn gushed. "You'd love it."

Finally, it sounded like Tanya had a chance to talk. She was about to speak when she heard the snap of a twig behind her. Before she could turn, she felt the tip of a gun barrel press against the back of her head.

"Don't move, and don't make a sound," a voice whispered.

Tanya froze.

A hand reached over her shoulder from behind, tapped the disconnect icon, yanked the phone out of her hand and let it drop to the ground.

The unseen person pressed the barrel even harder against the back of her head. "Move."

On shaky legs, Tanya walked into the forest.

FOUR

"**D**ispatch, this is 25-6. We're in the area and can respond to the report of a possible abduction of an adult female at gunpoint."

"Copy, 25-6. I show you en route."

Danny was already accelerating up the long driveway to the house where Tanya and Calvin were staying when he heard the transmission of a second responding patrol over his police scanner.

Anxiety gripped his gut as he thought about Tanya and Calvin enduring another terrifying attack. They'd already been through so much trauma. It didn't seem fair. But then, so much in life didn't seem fair. He saw a lot of the fallout from trauma and hurt in his line of work.

When he first started up the drive, there were pine trees close to the edge of it, but then the narrow road curved and the landscape opened to offer a view of a brightly colored house at least a hundred years old with gables and peaks and multiple chimneys with wisps of smoke lifting out of two of them.

There was an expanse of lawn behind the house, and beyond that were rows of apple trees looking spindly and losing their leaves now that harvesttime had passed. There were other structures on the property besides the house, including a red-and-white barn with a matching stable and a blue metal storage shed. Beside the shed, not far from the trees marking the beginning of the forest, sat Tanya's sedan. It was parked on a square of crushed rock strewn with a few curled brown leaves. There was nobody in or around it.

Tanya. Already, he felt a connection to her. Almost as if they'd been friends over the last twelve years. They hadn't been, of course, but the feeling was still there. Responding to the emergency call as soon as he heard it was not simply one more step in an attempt to do his job and track down a bail jumper. Instead, he felt an intense need to help someone close to him.

The first step was to respond to whoever had made the 9-1-1 call reporting that someone was in danger. Danny steered toward the house and slammed on the brakes when he reached the end of the short walkway that led to the steps of the wide wraparound porch at the front of the residence.

The lavender door with a frosted-glass oval in the center was flung open. A man who looked to be in his midsixties, with salt-and-pepper hair and wearing a thick gray pullover sweater, stormed out carrying a rifle across his chest. A blonde woman of similar age, also bundled up and carrying a rifle, followed him out the front door. She took several steps and then stopped in a stance that signaled she wasn't about to let anyone get past her. The man continued walking, heading in Danny's direction.

Danny slid out of his SUV and hurried around it to talk to the guy, hoping to get a quick summary of what had happened.

The man stopped, lifted the rifle to his shoulder and took aim at Danny. "Stop right there!"

Of course. The guy had no idea who Danny was or why he was here. He was understandably nervous since something bad had just happened.

Avoiding any sudden moves, Danny slowly lifted his hands. He identified himself and explained that he was nearby because he'd followed Tanya from her office to make sure she arrived safely. "I heard a dispatch go out over my police scanner," he said. "I'm here to help. Please, tell me what happened. Where is Tanya?"

"Let's just wait for the police to arrive," the man said without lowering his rifle.

Danny fought to get a handle on his impatience. He wanted to yell *No! In an abduction, every second counts, and we can't afford to waste any time!* But pushing the guy might make things worse. Sometimes trying to rush things actually made them progress more slowly. A reality that Danny found very challenging. He made himself take a deep breath before he spoke, and in the process, he noticed movement by a house window. A familiar young boy stood there.

"Calvin," he said. Keeping his hands up, he gave the boy a slight wave. Calvin waved back. "See, he knows me," Danny said. "We met last night in the middle of a pretty dire situation. Later, he and his aunt and I spent some time together over dinner. Tanya must have mentioned something about that. You must be her uncle

Matt. And that must be her aunt Winnie up there on the porch."

"Yeah, I'm Matt." The man lowered his rifle slightly, but he still kept it pointed in Danny's direction. "And she mentioned the name Danny Ryan. Can you prove that's who you are?"

"Sure. Let me show you my ID. I'm going to reach into my pocket, but I'll move slowly." This whole slow-going thing was agonizing, but they were nearly to the point where these people would trust him.

"Tell me about the abduction," Danny said as he pulled out his wallet and flipped it open so Matt could see his driver's license.

Matt moved closer and peered at it. "My wife saw what happened." He finally lowered his rifle and waved the woman over. "Honey, this is Danny, the bounty hunter Tanya was talking about. Tell him what you saw."

"I can't tell you much," Winnie said, her voice trembling and her eyes shiny with fear. "I knew Tanya was leaving work early and coming back here, so I kept an eye out for her. I heard her car drive past the house and I kept expecting to hear her walk in the door. Finally, I looked out the window and—" There was a catch in her voice, and she started to break down in tears. She bit down on her lips to collect herself, and then took a steadying breath. "I saw her walking into the woods. There were two men behind her, one of them close enough to hold a gun to her head.

"Their backs were turned to me, so I couldn't see their faces." Winnie sniffed loudly. "I yelled for Matt. We didn't dare run out there for fear somebody would come in the house to grab Calvin. So we called the police. They should be here any minute." She glanced back at Calvin, as if wanting to confirm that he was still standing there at the window.

"Where exactly did Tanya walk into the forest?"

Winnie turned back around from checking on her grandnephew and pointed to the tree line, not far from Tanya's parked car. Danny started running in that direction, slowing only when he reached the end of the grassy area to look for footprints to see if he could pick up a trail. Since it was a group of three people, they'd left tracks that were easy to spot. At least initially.

Everyone in the Ryan family volunteered with Range River Search and Rescue. Danny had good training in tracking someone who was lost in the forest. Further experience as a bounty hunter had taught him a few things when going after someone randomly running from arrest. In that case, a person tended to choose each option in front of them based on what was easiest and would get them the greatest distance the fastest. People on the run usually headed toward flat surfaces, moved downhill if they could and, when possible, they completely avoided large obstacles like boulders or fallen trees.

The route of escape taken by someone attempting to flee after committing a planned crime could have a different dynamic. Their choices could be motivated by a goal of getting to some predetermined point, like a place to rendezvous with accomplices, or a spot where they intended to pick up a vehicle that had been left for them. The possibility that they were trying to return to a car hidden nearby seemed highly probable since Matt and Winnie hadn't pointed out a strange vehicle on their property, and Danny hadn't seen anybody parked on the side of the road or along the driveway leading up to the house.

Thanks to the rain last night that had left the soil slightly damp, Danny was at first able to pick out the trail where Tanya and the abductors had walked fairly easily. Farther into the woods, where the trees were thicker, there was a deep layer of pine needles on the ground. The trail became less obvious then, and he wasn't able to follow it as quickly.

His heart pounded in his chest, less from exertion and more from fear. The thugs— and he was pretty certain they were the same two from the attack last night— could force Tanya to go in any direction. He couldn't know for certain why they'd grabbed her, and he hoped they meant to keep her alive to get whatever information it was they were so desperate to have from her sister. But maybe not—maybe they intended to kill Tanya to send a terrifying message to Dawn.

Danny reached an outcropping of rock and realized he'd completely lost the trail. He knew to pick it up again by circling the perimeter of the outcropping, searching for footprints in the surrounding soil, but that would take time he didn't have. Time the thugs could use to get away.

Dear Lord, help! he prayed silently.

Sight was not the only sense he had to pick up a trail. Much as he felt compelled to keep moving, he made himself stop for a moment. He needed to be completely silent and listen for sounds in the forest.

He gave it a few seconds, his chest tightening as he fought to not give up hope. And then, finally, he heard something. A male voice, though he couldn't understand the specific words, followed by the sounds of twigs and small branches snapping.

Wailing police sirens blasted up the hill toward the house behind him, ruining his chances of hearing any other subtle sounds, but at least he'd heard enough to know which way to go. As he started moving, he began thinking about what was in the immediate vicinity, and he remembered a small public park with picnic tables and barbecue pits set alongside a rocky, meandering stream.

That park had a parking lot. Was it possible that bail jumper Victor had stolen yet another car and left it there so he and his partner could escape with their captive?

He couldn't be certain. And even if his hunch was right, he still might not get to them in time to rescue Tanya. It crossed his mind to try to call the cops and alert them. He glanced around, wondering if a call would even connect out here.

It had sounded like Tanya and her captors weren't too far away. Rather than slow down and try to make the call, risking that the criminals would get away, Danny decided to double down on his plan to intercept them. He began to run faster, praying that he wasn't making a terrible mistake.

Tanya's head spun in what felt like a slow, wobbling motion. Her temples pounded, and her stomach felt like it had lurched halfway up into her throat. Her eyelids started to flutter open, but then the vivid memory of being taken at gunpoint flashed across her mind, and something told her to be careful. Someone could be watching her, and having them mistakenly believe she was still unconscious could work to her advantage.

She lay still for a moment. *Lord, I know You're here even if I can't feel Your presence,* she prayed silently. The truth was she felt very alone and afraid and confused. Slowly, she knitted together snippets of memory. Of walking downhill, which made sense. Uncle Matt and Aunt Winnie's home and the apple orchard were on top of a hill. She remembered that there was a second assailant besides the one who'd pressed the barrel of a gun to her head. She remembered the kidnappers calling a halt to their march in the forest. Shortly after that, she'd felt a sudden flash of pain at the back of her head.

She'd been knocked unconscious.

Why hadn't they killed her?

Maybe they planned to eventually. Maybe they planned to use her instead of Calvin to get whatever information they wanted from Dawn. And if their plan didn't work—or even if it *did*—what would they do with her? Maybe they'd let her go. Maybe not. Victor Durbin's still-unidentified accomplice had recklessly fired shots out the back window of their getaway car last night, obviously not caring one bit who might get hurt or killed.

These likely weren't people who spent much time pondering the sanctity of life. That meant if killing her was the most convenient thing to do, they would probably do it. She had no way of knowing for sure, but she couldn't afford to take any chances. She had to do something to try and save herself.

Dear Lord, please guide me.

Her thoughts focused on a sound she'd

been vaguely aware of since she'd gained consciousness. A low sound, like water gurgling in a stream. When she paid attention to it, she realized what she heard was voices. Three different voices. Victor the bail jumper and his accomplice, plus somebody else.

She listened closely, trying to make sense of what they said. She heard words, but it was hard to piece them together. They were in the middle of a conversation that didn't make sense.

Her thoughts shifted to the realization that they were several feet away from her, and while they were talking, they were probably facing each other. This might be her chance to open her eyes without any of them noticing.

She lifted her lids slightly, grateful they hadn't blindfolded her, and peered through her eyelashes.

As she'd suspected, the three men stood several feet away, and for the moment, their attention was focused on one another. She saw the two men she recognized from the attack last night. She couldn't see the face of the third man. She could only see that he wore a stylish, expensive-looking leather jacket and nice slacks.

Her hammering heart sent her pulse slamming against every bone in her chest as she opened her eyes a little wider and looked around. She also tried moving her hands and feet a little and was surprised to find them free and unbound.

The kidnappers thought she wasn't a threat. Since her legs weren't all that long and she wasn't exactly skinny, they'd likely assumed she couldn't outrun them. That might be true, but it was also true that she wasn't a quitter. And she was not about to let them use her to get to Calvin, if that was their ultimate goal.

She didn't dare move her head much to look around, but maybe she didn't need to. It appeared that she was near the bottom of the hill where the land flattened out and stretched toward the park.

Running for the park seemed like it would make her an easy target. The city kept the trees thinned out down there so people would have room to set up volley-ball nets or play soccer or whatever. The bad guys would see her and outrun her and catch her for sure.

It would make more sense to use the cover of the forest. She would get up and run and hide and circle her way around until she got back up the hill to the house. She'd done something similar—a kind of extreme hide-and-seek—countless times when she was a kid playing with her cous-ins and her sister.

If she was going to do anything, she needed to do it now, before the thugs stopped talking and turned their atten-tion to her.

Too late.

Victor looked directly at her, his gaze

fixed, as if he'd figured out that she was awake. She forced a quick, deep breath, shoved herself to her feet and started running.

The sudden movement made her head swim violently, and she took uneven, staggering, time-wasting steps.

No! At this rate it wouldn't take them more than a couple of minutes to grab her, knock her out again and probably tie her up this time. If they didn't kill her.

Behind her, she could hear them yelling, but she couldn't risk looking back. Instead, she tried to run uphill, away from the men, desperate to put as much distance as she could between herself and them.

She knew better than to run in a straight line. Instead, she tried to zig and zag at irregular intervals, using the trees for cover as much as she could.

Gunfire suddenly erupted. Tanya heard bullets whizzing by, followed by the sounds of cracks and splintering as they hit the trees beside and ahead of her. Terrified, she dived for cover behind a fallen tree.

One of the bad guys yelled—it sounded like the man she'd never seen before today—and the shooting stopped.

She saw a flicker of movement uphill a few paces away, and her heart sank. One of the criminals must have gotten ahead of her. She was already surrounded. Her escape had barely even started, and she was about to be recaptured.

The flicker of movement became just a little bit more pronounced, and she saw it was not one of the bad guys. It was Danny Ryan standing behind a tree.

He had a pistol in his hand, and as he stayed mostly hidden, he gestured at her to remain where she was hunkered down behind the fallen tree.

Tanya took a breath. Her throat was so dry from fear that it felt like the air scratched all the way down to her lungs. She dared to glance behind her and saw the criminals through the trees. Victor and his bald companion were close, guns in hand, moving slowly, turning their heads side to side as if they weren't sure in which direction she'd gone. Their newer accomplice was farther back, barely visible and not joining in the search.

She heard the rustle of dead leaves and dried pine needles moving and turned around just as Danny hurried over the deadfall and dropped to the ground beside her.

"Are you all right?" he whispered.

She nodded, because at first she couldn't speak. Fear for her life had given her an almost numbing sense that what was happening right now could not be real. One minute she was an accountant with a quiet life. And the next, people were trying to kidnap her nephew, chasing her through the forest and trying to *kill* her.

"I'll be okay," she finally whispered, because he was staring at her as if the nod wasn't enough and he was waiting for actual words. She couldn't actually say she was okay, because she wasn't. She *really* wasn't.

Victor and his accomplice were on them in an instant. Danny sprang to his feet and pointed his gun at the assailants. Tanya, still unsteady, got to her feet as quickly as she could.

"Drop your gun," Victor said to Danny.

The bounty hunter lifted his chin slightly. "No."

"Drop it or we'll shoot *her*." Victor gestured toward Tanya with his chin.

"If you were going to shoot her, you would have done that already," Danny said. "You must need her alive. Or someone told you to take her alive."

Their words made Tanya feel even queasier.

Victor waved his gun in Danny's direction. "Maybe I'll just shoot you."

"Are you truly that stupid?" Danny asked.

Tanya's jaw dropped. *Really?* Danny was going to antagonize a man pointing a gun at him and threatening to kill him? And yet, why was she surprised? People didn't change. Life had taught her that. And clearly, Danny was the same impulsive wiseacre he'd been when they were in high school.

"I called the cops the second I spotted you guys down here," Danny continued, sounding more annoyed than concerned. "I'm sure your gunshots have already helped them narrow down exactly where we are. And, of course, I gave them your name, Victor. They'll be here any minute."

Tanya was afraid he was bluffing. But in the few beats of silence that followed, she could hear faint voices and a dog barking excitedly. *Please let that be a K-9 tracking dog.*

"I saw somebody else out here when I first spotted you two. Your friend or boss or whatever he is has already abandoned you. But hey, stick around and wait for the cops if you want."

"Is that true?" Victor said to his accomplice.

The bald guy kept his gun pointed at Tanya but took a quick glance downhill. "Yeah. Looks like he's gone."

The sounds of the cops and their barking, baying K-9 grew louder. They were getting closer.

Victor slowly backed up. His accomplice did the same. Both of them kept their guns trained on Danny and Tanya until at last they turned and disappeared into the forest.

"Thank You, Lord," Tanya said quietly.

"Amen," Danny agreed.

Despite her sense of relief, Tanya's trembling knees began to shake even harder. Right this second, standing here beside Danny with cops on their way, she felt safe. In the larger scale of things, when she considered how her life might play out in the next hours and days and weeks, she didn't feel safe at all.

FIVE

"I was born and raised in this town," Tanya said. "And this is the first time I've been inside the police department."

Danny shifted his gaze to her hazel eyes. They were more brown than green, he decided. He took in the red marks on the side of her face and on her collarbones visible near the neckline of her shirt. Those marks would turn darker as the day wore on and be ugly bruises by tomorrow. Reminders of a nightmare experience she should not have been forced to endure.

At least the doctor at the urgent care clinic inside the county hospital had been able to confirm that she had no fractures or subdural bleeding or any other life-threatening injuries. The dizziness she'd been experiencing when he first found her had subsided, but the doctor still warned her to take it easy for the next couple of weeks.

"I suppose I should be grateful that I've made it this long—well, until yesterday, at least—without needing help from law enforcement," she muttered.

"We're going to find all three of those creeps." Danny leaned toward her in the visitor's chair beside him and rested his fingertips across her hand where it gripped the arm of the chair so tightly that her knuckles were white.

The impulse to take her whole hand in his was there. He wanted to try and offer her some sense of certainty or comfort, but he didn't give in to the inclination.

Despite the emotional intensity of the last twenty-one hours, the danger and fear for her life, and the fact that they'd known each other in high school, they were still practically strangers. Beyond that, he didn't want to give her the wrong idea. It was his job to catch bad guys and protect people. His reassurances to her would be given in a professional capacity; they would not be personal. Though they might seem like it.

Not personal at all, he reminded himself as he removed his hand and leaned back in his chair. He might be feeling a little nostalgia at seeing an old acquaintance from high school, but that was it. He would feel the same empathy for anyone in her situation.

"All right, I've got some mug shots for you both to look at." Detective Romanov strode into the room carrying an electronic tablet. "I need you to move your chairs apart and look at the photos separately," she said. "So you don't influence one another."

"Will these potentially be pictures of

Victor Durbin's accomplice in the attack at my house?" Tanya asked. "Or will it be the third man who was in the forest? The one in the leather jacket."

The detective gave her a cool glance before saying, "It's up to you to tell me who you see."

"It goes back to not wanting to influence what we say," Danny explained to Tanya when she looked nonplussed at the detective's response. Romanov could be a little contrary to work with sometimes, but Danny had come to realize that it was because she took her job very seriously. "It does little good to capture a suspect if there's no criminal conviction at the end of it all because some step along the way allows for the case to be dismissed."

The detective spared a glance for Danny. While he couldn't exactly say she smiled at him, she did give him a microscopic nod that bordered on indicating approval. That was something.

Tanya looked at the photos first, quickly swiping through several until she suddenly stopped. Danny couldn't see the image, but he could see Tanya's eyes getting big. "This is him, the man who was with Victor when they invaded my house," she said to Romanov, her tone sounding startled and indignant at the same time. She turned to the detective. "Who is this creep?"

"Look at the rest of the pictures," Romanov said evenly.

Tanya swiped several more times, but she didn't see any other images she recognized.

It was Danny's turn next, and he was anxious to start looking. He'd already sent out a description of Victor Durbin's accomplice to his informants and fellow bounty hunters in the region, hoping someone would recognize the thug. So far, no one had.

After looking at several dozen photos,

including pictures of criminals he recognized from other cases, he came across the photo of Victor's balding, heavyset friend.

"Who is this guy?" Danny asked. "Is he from around here?" If he was a local, Danny had a good shot at getting some helpful information on him by asking around town.

"His name is Max Curry," Romanov said, taking the tablet from Danny and walking around to sit in the chair behind her desk. "Seattle PD has asked us to keep an eye out for him. He's out on bond for felony assault. He skipped his court date, and his credit card trail indicates he's been in Range River for a couple of weeks. Unfortunately, the records don't give us a hotel or any other location where he may be staying."

"So he's a bail jumper," Danny said. "Along with Victor." Danny could contact the company that bonded Max Curry and offer to make the recovery for them. That should in turn lead to that bail bonds company giving Danny all the information they had about violent Max.

Romanov gave Danny another tight nod of her head. "Looks like it would be good for us to continue to work together on this," she said. "But don't get in the way."

Danny didn't bother trying to hold back the wide grin that flashed across his lips. This was a milestone moment in working with Detective Romanov. He couldn't wait to tell everyone at Range River Bail Bonds he'd actually been invited by Romanov to work with her on a case.

Of course, the detective did not return his smile. Instead, she shook her head and turned her attention to the laptop on her desk.

Danny quickly swiped through the rest of the photos. He figured doing that would make the typically thorough detective happy. He set the tablet on the corner of her desk when he was done. "I didn't see a photo of anyone I think might be the third man, either. Though, like I told you, I didn't get much of a look at him."

"Okay," the detective said smoothly. A moment later, her eyes still on the laptop screen and not gazing directly at Tanya, she said, "Have you heard anything more from your sister?"

Her tone sounded casual, almost distracted, but Danny knew better. He was also anxious for a chance to talk to Dawn Rivera, to see if a conversation with her could bring to light a motive for the attacks. Like the detective, he figured that direct questions about Dawn would bring out a defensive streak in Tanya. He could understand that. He had a base-level instinct to protect his brother and sister. Wade, too, since he was pretty much an adopted brother. And even when he thought his siblings were in the wrong, if he felt like they were under attack, his initial response was to protect them in front of everyone else and pull them aside and give them what for later.

Tanya sighed, ran her hands through her dark blond hair and slouched a little in her chair. "Dawn told me that after Victor grabbed my phone and disconnected the call, she tried to call me back. When she couldn't get me, she eventually called Aunt Winnie, who decided to tell her everything about what was going on. That might have been the best thing to do. I don't know. Anyway, it's still tough to move around outside the resort where Dawn is staying because of the damage from the storm, but she told Aunt Winnie she's going to figure out a way to get home as soon as she can."

"I'd like to speak with her when she gets here," Romanov said.

Me, too, Danny thought and nodded.

"Of course."

"How's your nephew?" the detective asked.

"He didn't see me taken away at gun-point, so that's good." Tanya shook her head. "That sweet kid doesn't need any more trauma. He's in the lobby with my aunt and uncle right now. I got a text from my aunt a short while ago. For his sake, they're trying to act normal. He said he was hungry earlier, so they walked with him to the bakery on the corner."

Tanya was quiet for a moment, and then Danny saw her eyes start to glisten and her cheeks and the tip of her nose turned red. "A little boy shouldn't have to go through something like this," she said, taking in a gasping breath between the last two words before tears started roll-ing down her cheeks.

Dear Lord, Danny prayed silently. He didn't add any more words, just left it at that because he was thinking of the many tragic situations he'd come across in his bounty-hunting career. Terrible stories.

There were people still fighting to recover even if the culprit responsible for their pain was locked up. He wanted to send a prayer up for all those people. He couldn't begin to put all his hopes for them into words, but he figured the Lord knew what was in his heart. And knew that his concerns included Tanya and Calvin.

The detective slid a box of tissues across her desk toward Tanya.

Danny mentally kicked himself for not thinking to grab the tissues for her himself.

Tanya pulled out several from the box and dabbed her eyes and nose.

"I'm sorry for what you and your family are going through," Romanov said.

While the detective wasn't displaying a lot of emotion, Danny thought she did sound sincere.

"I can assure you that the Range River Police Department is doing everything we can to find the assailants, but I obviously can't promise you that there won't be more attacks."

Tanya visibly drew in a breath, as if trying to fortify herself.

"Are you and your nephew going to stay with your aunt and uncle again tonight? If so, I'll have a patrol car stationed out there."

"I don't know what to do," Tanya said. "The people behind these attacks are obviously desperate. We don't know who one of them is, and we don't even know what they ultimately want." She turned to Danny, her eyes widening with increasing fear. "If I go back up to the farm, the thugs might figure out some way to sneak around any cop parked outside and get into the house. They might do something horrible to Aunt Winnie and Uncle Matt to silence them. And what about Calvin?

Today, the kidnappers went after me. What if they've changed their minds for some reason and I'm their new target instead of him? What if staying close to my nephew will put him in greater danger?"

She tilted her head back and looked up at the ceiling, exhaling a deep breath. "Lord, what do I do?"

Danny didn't think for a minute that he was the answer to her prayers, but he did have an idea.

"Given that this is a dangerous and unpredictable situation," he said, "I'd like to make an unusual suggestion."

Tanya turned to him. "Go ahead."

"My brother, Connor, owns the old Riverside Inn. He remodeled it and turned it into a private residence with several rooms. You and Calvin could stay there. For the time being, I could stay there, too. So could Hayley and Wade. Wade's mom works with us, so she'd probably stay, as well."

Tanya tilted her head, a doubtful expression on her face.

"Range River Bail Bonds has an office downtown," he continued. "Connor never has clients come to the inn, but since there are people with grudges against him who might know where he lives, the security's very good. All of us would do our best to keep you safe."

Tanya turned to the detective. "What do you think?"

Romanov cocked a slender auburn eyebrow. "You and your nephew staying in a relatively fortified building surrounded by bounty hunters determined to protect you? Right now, I think that's exactly what you need."

"Okay." Tanya turned to Danny. "Let's go."

"It's been a while since I've been in this part of town," Tanya said. "The last time I saw the Riverside Inn, the windows were boarded up, the gardens were overgrown with pine saplings and blackberry vines had taken over most of the old dirt pathways."

She stood in the middle of a cleanly swept walkway made of red brick that led from the parking lot to the inn's main entrance. Her gaze settled for a moment on the imposing ten-foot-tall door in front of her.

The north side of the inn aligned with the river. Made of stone and heavy timber, the inn still had the feel of the transit point it had been for travelers and traders heading along the waterway or crossing it back in the early twentieth century. At the same time, it was obvious, even to someone just standing outside, that it had been restored and updated with new windows and doors, a sturdy pitched roof designed to avoid a heavy accumulation of snow, plenty of outside light fixtures, and a security system with cameras staged to

cover the main building and nearby parking area. For all Tanya knew, there were
cameras on the few acres of property that
surrounded the inn, as well.

She turned and glanced over at Calvin,
who was of course already off the walkway and wandering in the dirt in a hap-
hazard pattern, probably following a bug
or some other creature.

"Connor's mother inherited this place
along with nearly enough money to ren-
ovate it just before she passed away,"
Danny said. He'd insisted on carrying
Tanya's and Calvin's suitcases. While
Tanya and Calvin had waited at the police station, her aunt and uncle had gone
back to their house to get their belongings
so they could have them to take to the inn.

"There was some kind of falling-out between his mom and her family when she
married our dad," he continued. "They
weren't interested in welcoming her
back into the family after she and Dad

divorced. She and Connor had a rough time." Danny cleared his throat. "Anyway, not long before she died, the family reached out to her. I'm not sure of the details. They gifted her this property and some cash, which she left to Connor."

"What about your dad?" Tanya asked. "You and Hayley and Connor share the same dad, right? Is he part of your organization?"

"He and my mom died when I was eleven," Danny said flatly.

Tanya glanced over at him, expecting further explanation. Instead, Danny simply held her gaze and kept his mouth shut. That was a significant act for a talkative guy like Danny.

"Connor and Hayley are working out of town right now," he said after a moment. "They're helping some bounty hunters from an agency south of here on a recovery. They should be back tomorrow."

"Well, this place is beautiful," Tanya said. "Thank you for inviting us here."

"It's our refuge." At the sound of light footfalls, he glanced back at Calvin, who had concluded his bug hunting or whatever he'd been doing. As soon as the boy caught up with them, Danny started walking toward the door, with Tanya and Calvin matching his pace.

"A refuge, huh?" Tanya said. "From the criminals you guys go out and hunt for?"

"Partly that. It's a place for us to come together as a family and remember that we have each other's backs when life takes us in different directions for too long and the connection between us starts to feel too thin. It's also a refuge for other people, because we haven't forgotten what it's like to feel as if you're flailing around in the world all on your own."

Given that Danny had family and ties to the community, his comment struck her as odd.

They stopped at the door, where he slid aside a metal covering and entered a series of numbers into a numeric keypad.

"What? No James Bond–style retinal scanner?" she asked.

Danny smiled at her as he reached to open the door. "We don't have James Bond's budget."

She stepped past him into a huge room with a high ceiling that stretched to the top of the second floor. Several amber-colored glass light fixtures hung from thick wooden support beams, looking like dangling jewels. Directly across from her was an oversize fireplace made of flat river stones, and on either side of the fireplace, floor-to-ceiling windows afforded a view of a wide wooden deck covering the ground next to the inn and extending out several feet over the river.

Through some passages on the first floor, she could glimpse part of a kitchen and dining area and a room that looked like an office or maybe a den. Staircases at either end of the great room led to an upstairs gallery that was apparently where the bedrooms were located.

The place managed to seem cozy and impressive at the same time. It kept a bit of the historical feel, including the fireplace with its low, flickering flames and mild campfire smell, but it also felt comfortably contemporary, right down to the glass-topped desk sitting off to one side with a desktop computer, four screens, a couple of cell phones and a tablet.

A dark-haired, dusky-skinned woman stood from the desk and walked toward Tanya with a smile on her face. She was maybe in her fifties—it was hard to say. She looked familiar, though at first Tanya couldn't figure out why.

"Welcome," the woman said, extending her hand to Tanya. "I'm Maribel Fast Horse. I believe you've met my son, Wade."

Ah, Wade's mom. That's why she looked familiar. "Pleased to meet you," Tanya said, shaking her hand. After she let go, she turned to Danny. "How many families are involved in your business?"

Danny flashed a smile at Maribel. "We like to think of ourselves as one family."

"Well, it's a big one," Tanya said.

"Wade and his mom lived on the street where we lived after our parents died and Connor took us in. The Fast Horses were going through a rough patch at the same time we were. We helped each other whenever we could, and we've never stopped doing that."

Tanya couldn't help thinking of her own family, of how alone and alienated she'd felt growing up when her parents split up and then got back together, only to do the whole thing over and over again. Her aunt and uncle were kind to her and Dawn, but they'd been busy raising their own two children at the time. There had only been so much they could do. It would have been nice to have a solid network to rely on back then, an extended family like the Ryans and Fast Horses.

A dog let out a couple of inquiring barks at the far end of the house from somewhere down a passage Tanya couldn't see into.

"Do you like dogs?" Maribel asked Calvin. "And cats?"

The boy nodded emphatically. He loved animals, and Dawn had mentioned getting him a dog or cat when he was a little older.

"Well, that's good," she continued. "Because we have dogs and cats here." Maribel turned to Tanya while Calvin practically danced with excitement. "He's not allergic to the animals?"

"No."

"Well, then I'm sure they'd all like to welcome you," Maribel said as she turned back to the boy. "I put them in a room with the door shut until I was certain it would be okay for you to meet them." She extended her hand toward him. "Would you like to help me set them loose to run around in the house?"

Calvin eagerly reached for her hand. "Yes!"

"Maribel helps with some of the online research we do, as well as the basic management side of the business. Plus, she takes care of the inn and oftentimes stays over to help when we have guests."

"So she doesn't usually live here?"

"She, Wade, Hayley and I all have our own places. When we have an intense case going on or there's some other reason we feel like we want to stick together, we usually all stay here. Otherwise, we stay in our own homes. Sometimes you can only stand so much togetherness before you need to get away," he said, adding a grin to soften his comment.

A moment later, Tanya heard excited

barking and the sound of Calvin laughing. Calvin trotted down the hallway in Tanya's direction with two dogs at his heels and four cats hugging the hallway walls before sprinting past him and bounding in different directions once they reached the great room.

Her nephew appeared lighthearted, at least for the moment, and she was glad.

Right now, they were safe.

She drew in a deep breath, blew it out and took yet another look around. This was a beautiful setting, complete with cute animals, and she was grateful for that. The truth was, as warm and cozy as it felt at the moment, the inn was a place for them to hide. She and Calvin were here because someone had tried to kidnap each of them. Maybe whoever was behind the attacks now planned to kill one or both of them. The kidnappers who'd come after her had not hesitated to fire potentially lethal shots.

A shiver passed over her skin despite the warmth emanating from the glowing flames in the fireplace. She and Calvin were still alive, but there were still so many terrifying unanswered questions swirling around them.

At least Calvin's mom would be arriving home tomorrow. That should make the boy feel better.

Sadly, Tanya was a little bit afraid that her sister's return to Range River might make things worse.

SIX

When Tanya opened her eyes the next morning, the back of her head where she'd been struck yesterday was sore.

She rolled over onto her side to see the clock on the nightstand, and it felt like she hit every one of the bruises she'd accumulated since the attacks started two days ago. At least right now she could see her nephew as he lay sound asleep in the rollaway bed beside her and know he was safe.

"Thank You, Lord," she prayed softly. Sometimes it was too easy to stay focused on what went wrong and forget to be grateful for what was going right. When the stakes were life and death, pressing into her faith and being mindful of her thinking took on a greater importance.

It was eight fifteen, well past the time she was normally up on a weekday. She'd already let her employer know she wouldn't be coming into the office today.

Calvin stirred under his blankets. Apparently, he'd slept through the night. She assumed if he'd woken or had bad dreams, she would have known about it. After dinner last night, he'd expressed concern about whether the *mean men* were going to come back and try to get him again, but at least he'd seemed to feel safe at the moment. She'd listened to him, reassured him with lots of hugs and kisses, and then let him watch a lighthearted children's movie until he fell asleep.

Tanya reached for her phone on the nightstand and powered it up. The police had been able to retrieve it from the spot where Victor had dropped it. Detective Romanov conjectured the thugs hadn't taken it because they were afraid of being tracked. The screen was cracked, but it was fine other than that. Last night, Tanya had turned it off before she plugged it in to charge it, figuring that she and Calvin both needed a night of uninterrupted sleep.

Her phone began chirping and beeping with various alerts. Her sister had called and texted her several times. She scrolled through Dawn's texts first. They contained the specifics of her return trip from Mexico, including the fact that she'd be arriving at the regional airport here in Range River shortly after 1:00 p.m. local time today. There were a few more texts from her after that, asking if everything was okay. Her tense voice mail messages all asked the same thing. Apparently, Dawn had worried throughout the night.

Tanya tried to call to reassure her sister, but the connection went directly to voice mail. There were numerous reasons why a person wouldn't be able to take a call when they were in transit, so Tanya tried not to worry that Dawn might be in trouble. Instead, she left a message telling her that Calvin was fine and everything was okay.

There was nothing new from Detective Romanov, so, ignoring the other messages for now, she got out of bed, grabbed some clothes from her suitcase and headed for the en suite bathroom to take a shower and get dressed. On her way, she pulled aside a curtain to look out the window at the river flowing steadily by and the cloud-topped mountain peaks in the distance.

Her room was on the second floor, near where Hayley and Maribel were staying. Danny and Wade were bunked in rooms at the other end of the inn. That was also the part of the inn where Connor Ryan normally stayed. The founder and owner of Range River Bail Bonds was supposed to return sometime this morning, along with Hayley, assuming they'd captured their bad guys.

After Tanya was dressed, she opened the bathroom door and purposefully made a lot of noise as she dried her hair and put on a touch of makeup, hoping to wake up Calvin slowly and easily. As she got ready, she used extra makeup to cover the bruises visible on the side of her face and her collarbone. The last thing she wanted was for Calvin to focus on them and get scared.

Her plan worked. By the time she was finished, Calvin wandered into the bathroom, rubbing his eyes and complaining that he was hungry. Tanya reached out to smooth down that stubborn tuft of hair that still refused to cooperate. Yesterday afternoon, when he'd been able to video chat with his mom, his hair had been sticking out in every direction.

"Your mom is on her way home," she

said, kissing the top of her nephew's head. "She'll be here today."

"Yay!" Calvin shouted, throwing up his arms.

Soon after, the boy was dressed and ready to greet the day. Maybe a little too ready. When Tanya opened the door to the hallway, he sprinted past her, let out a whoop and yelled, "Doggies!" as he raced toward the stairs.

There was a chorus of barks in response, and the sound of scrambling dog toenails down on the first floor.

Tanya let out a sigh, sincerely hoping that everyone else in the house was already awake. While slowly walking down the stairs, figuring there must be aspirin or something similar in the house to help with the aches and pains, she heard Calvin greeting the dogs. Nearing the bottom steps, she caught a whiff of coffee. That might help with her headache. And she smelled bacon and fried potatoes and onions, too.

While Calvin rolled around on the floor of the great room with his new canine buddies, Tanya followed her nose into the spacious kitchen that extended into a dining area with a bay window facing the river. A half-filled coffeepot on the counter called to her like a beacon.

Maribel saw her and stepped away from the stove and the cast-iron pan full of potatoes and onions she was monitoring. She opened a cabinet door, pulled out a mug, filled it and held it toward Tanya.

"Thank you," Tanya said, reaching for it. There were cream and sugar on the counter, but Tanya preferred her coffee black.

"Do you have any aspirin?" she asked, and then took a sip of coffee.

Maribel reached into a different cabinet for a bottle of pain pills and set it on the counter in front of Tanya. Then she fetched her a glass, filled it with water and set that beside the bottle.

Tanya let go of the coffee mug just long enough to pick up the tablets and down them with some water. After that, she took a couple more sips of coffee and finally felt ready to face whatever the day might throw at her. She sighed deeply.

"Good morning," Maribel said with a mellow smile. "I hope you slept well."

In Tanya's opinion, the fact that the lady had waited until she'd gotten her coffee and her bearings before engaging her in conversation spoke volumes about the compassion in Maribel's heart. She smiled at her. "Good morning. We both slept great."

"Happy to hear it. Breakfast is almost ready. Take a seat at the table. Connor made it back early this morning. I don't believe you two have met. Of course, Hayley came with him."

Tanya took a few steps and turned toward the farmhouse-style table and the people sitting around it.

Danny's gaze was locked on her, his eyebrows lifted slightly, a questioning expression on his face. "How'd Calvin do last night?"

"Slept like a log." She took a sip of coffee and tried to ignore the unexpected ripple of delight she felt at seeing the bounty hunter sitting there, freshly shaved, in jeans and a nice long-sleeved dress shirt. "He's full of energy, and he'll probably exhaust your dogs today," she added.

"That'll be good for them." The comment came from the only unfamiliar face at the table. The speaker, a dark-haired man with coffee-colored eyes, stood as Tanya approached the table. As did everyone else. The gesture seemed a bit formal, but it was also nice.

"I'm Connor Ryan. We're glad to have you stay with us." He extended his hand, and Tanya shook it.

"Tanya Rivera. Pleased to meet you. And thank you for letting Calvin and me stay here."

"Happy to help," he said politely.

He looked a good ten years older than Danny. Maybe more. They were about the same height, but he had a slightly heavier build. He didn't appear to have Danny's nervous energy, but that could be because he'd apparently been out working most of the night. Though he seemed polite and kind, he definitely didn't have Danny's quick smile.

Tanya shifted her gaze to Hayley, and the Ryan sister gave her a small wave.

Finally, she looked over at Wade. There was a hint of mischief in his dark brown eyes. "I hope you're not on some kind of low-carb, low-fat diet," he said. "Because my mom doesn't know how to cook that kind of stuff."

"You seem to pack away my cooking

pretty good there, boy," his mom called over from her spot in front of the stove.

"I am definitely not complaining," he called back.

"Sit down." Danny pulled out a chair for Tanya. "I'll get Calvin."

Wade went to help his mother carry the platters of potatoes, scrambled eggs with cheese and warm biscuits to the table.

Danny returned with Calvin, who sat beside Tanya. Once everything was ready, they all held hands, and Hayley spoke a prayer of gratitude. Then they dug in.

"Dawn will be arriving home today a little after one in the afternoon," Tanya said after they were a few minutes into the meal.

Each of the bounty hunters shifted their gaze to her. They watched her intently, as if she'd sounded some kind of alert. She knew it was because they were all anxious to talk to Dawn, to hear what kind of story she might have to tell. None of them, Tanya included, were completely certain yet that the attacks hadn't been triggered by something that had happened to Dawn in Mexico. It was entirely possible she was hiding something or that, for some reason, she didn't want to speak frankly over the phone. Dawn was the key to getting a good lead so they could get busy bounty hunting.

"I'll pick her up at the airport and bring her directly here," Tanya added before taking a bite of a buttered biscuit. She'd driven her own car from the police station to the inn, with Danny following behind. She'd considered leaving her car at her aunt and uncle's so that it wouldn't be obvious where she was staying. But the bad guys already knew she was getting help from Danny and the rest of the Range River Bail Bonds crew, so they could easily guess where she was staying. While the attacks admittedly made Tanya look for protection, they also made her determined to keep some control of her own life. Just a few minutes as a hostage had made that a high priority. Reasonable or not, having her car felt like independence and freedom to her.

"I can drive over to the airport and get Dawn while you and Calvin stay here and relax," Danny said.

"That's great." Tanya nodded. "Thank you for offering to drive, but I'll go with you. I don't know what kind of state of mind my sister will be in." She glanced at Calvin, who was focused on getting a chunk of fried potato from the tine of his fork into his mouth. She wanted to be cautious of what she said in front of him. "Even if I send her a picture of you and tell her it's okay to go with you, she might not want to get into a vehicle with someone she doesn't actually know."

"All right," Danny said before scooping up another forkful of potatoes.

Tanya wiped the biscuit crumbs from

her hands, glad that she'd already eaten her fill, because the more she thought about talking to her sister in person, the more her stomach began to tumble nervously. She wanted to learn the truth from Dawn, but at the same time, she wasn't looking forward to hearing it. Dawn hadn't made the best decisions in the past. When she was younger, she'd dabbled in drugs and made friends with some very unsavory people along the way. Maybe she'd fallen back into old habits that had brought her in contact with criminals.

People don't change.

The prospect of questioning Dawn felt a little like turning over a big rock. Tanya needed to prepare herself to deal with whatever crawled out from underneath it.

Dawn Rivera clutched her son tightly. Calvin, who'd seemed so remarkably stoic after the attack on him, had burst into wracking sobs at the first sight of his mom. Even now, twenty minutes after Dawn had stepped into the main reception area of the regional airport, Calvin was still crying and shaking with his face pressed into his mother's neck.

Danny watched them. He'd had no idea the little guy had been bottling up such a storm of painful emotions. He should have done something to help the kid, but he had no idea what that might have been.

How did parents know the right thing to do for their children? There were moments when Danny saw families and thought he would like to have a family of his own one day, but then he'd think about the fact that he barely remembered his own dad. He really only knew how to be a brother. What if he had a kid and messed things up while trying to raise him or her?

Hayley stepped up beside him, interrupting his thoughts. "I'll grab Dawn's suitcase so we can get going." She glanced toward the floor-to-ceiling windows behind them. Beyond was a sidewalk and then a road that wrapped around the small airport and led to the highway. This was not a safe spot for Dawn—or any of them—to linger. Anyone who might have tailed the bounty hunters hoping to eventually find either of the Rivera sisters would be able to drive by and see them clearly. Maybe even fire a shot at one or both of them. Since the motivation behind the attacks was still a mystery, they couldn't rule out the possibility that whoever was behind them would intensify their actions from kidnapping to murder.

Introductions had already been made, so when Hayley walked toward Dawn to speak to her and reach for the handle of her suitcase, Dawn nodded in response and followed her. Calvin remained in his mother's arms.

Tanya stood a couple of feet away from Danny, twisting her hands together, her expression pinched. She looked desperate to step in and do something to make her nephew feel better. She had already hugged her sister, with Calvin in between her and Dawn, and she looked anxious to do it again.

"We need to get everybody back to the house," Danny said to her.

Tanya nodded. "Of course."

They moved toward the exit, where Wade had positioned himself so that he'd have the best view of people coming in and out of the building. As they headed in his direction, he stepped out in front of them and exited toward the parking lot and the two SUVs they'd driven to the airport. Danny dropped back so that Hayley, the two Rivera women and Calvin were in the middle of their small group.

A jet roared down the runway and rose into the air. "Look," Dawn said, gently lifting her son's head away from her neck and pointing in the direction of the aircraft. "Flying on a plane is so exciting. Don't you want to try it?"

After a moment's hesitation, Calvin nodded his head slightly.

"Well, guess what? Mom's going to take you on a plane ride tomorrow!"

What?

Tanya was walking ahead of Danny, and she stumbled slightly. She turned to her sister, and Danny could see the surprised and questioning expression on her face. Dawn only had eyes for her son, and she either didn't see Tanya or pretended not to. Tanya glanced over her shoulder at Danny. He returned her gaze and raised his eyebrows slightly so she'd know he'd overheard Dawn's comment, but he kept his mouth shut, determined not to jump into a conversation until they were safely in his SUV and on their way to the inn.

"So, California?" Tanya said brightly a few minutes later when they were traveling down the highway with Hayley and Wade following them.

Danny glanced over at Tanya. She was beside him in the front passenger seat but had twisted partly around so that she could see Dawn and Calvin in the back. Her face was flushed, and her jawline looked tense. Her tightly pressed lips made it clear she was trying to sound upbeat for her nephew's sake, but she had been taken aback by her sister's announcement and was none too happy about it.

"You remember my friend Valerie," Dawn said. "She moved down to California after she got married a couple of years ago. While I was waiting in the airport in Cozumel, I called her to see if Calvin and I could come for a visit, and she said yes."

Danny's thoughts kicked into overdrive as he scanned the road ahead of them. How many friends had Dawn called? What had she told them about the kidnapping attempt on Calvin as well as the attack on Tanya in the forest? And exactly who knew she would be taking her son to California? Once you gave information to a person, you had no control over whomever else they wanted to share it with. What if someone connected to the attack was a friend of a friend and they ended up hearing about Dawn's plans? She was plainly the main target, but the thugs were obviously willing to use her son if they needed to. Mother and son would be vulnerable in California with no one by their side who was willing and able to stop the bad guys.

Danny's body tightened with the effort to keep his mouth shut. Dawn was already talking to her son about the fun things they could do on their little vacation, and the boy was giggling with excitement. It was good to hear Calvin's happiness after he'd been so distraught just a short time ago. Danny was still dying to talk to Dawn about whether this was a good idea.

He would have to wait until they got to the house and the boy was out of earshot. And he would have to steel himself for the possibility that she'd tell him to mind his own business. That would be the hardest part. Not because he was thin-skinned, but because he'd already grown surprisingly attached to Calvin, even though he'd only known the kid a few days.

Tanya had already turned back around in her seat so that she was now facing forward, arms crossed tightly over her chest.

"Where exactly are we going?" Dawn asked when they reached the edge of town and kept to the old highway that paralleled the Range River. "Why didn't we make the turn back there?"

"We're going to stay with Danny and his family," Tanya said. "I told you that, remember? Calvin's already made a lot of friends there. The doggies love him."

Again, the lilt to her tone, obviously intended to keep Calvin from being alarmed, was in sharp contrast to her body language. Danny glanced at her again and saw her chin tucked down slightly toward her chest, as if she were bracing for a fight.

"I remember" came the reply from the back seat. "But I need to go home so I can grab some of Calvin's things."

"Aunt Winnie will get whatever you want from your house and bring it to you," Tanya said. "That way, you and Calvin won't be so visible in town."

They passed the cluster of trees alongside the river that marked the end of a public park, and shortly after that, Danny made the turn onto a curving drive that took them into the clearing where they could see the dramatic front entrance to the inn.

"Wow," Dawn said. "The last time I saw this old place, it was vacant and overgrown with vines. People thought it was going to be condemned. It looks gorgeous now. And it's your brother's house?"

"Connor likes to think it's his house," Danny responded, realizing her question had been directed at him. "But Hayley and I think of it as ours, too. So does Wade. So do a few other friends. We all have our own homes, but sometimes it just feels good to be here." *And it's safe.*

Connor might grumble about having people underfoot all the time, but nobody took his complaints seriously. Besides, it was his own fault. He invited people over, fed them and let them stay. He'd started out rescuing his siblings and ended up wanting to rescue seemingly everybody. Connor, Hayley and Wade were all the same—they all knew what it was like to live through hard times and how important any offer of forgiveness or assistance could be.

As soon as they parked, Danny sent Wade a text asking him to distract Calvin as quickly as possible. The boy's mom and Tanya needed to have a frank conversation—one Danny intended to listen in on—about what Dawn and Calvin would do next.

Wade bounded over as Danny was grabbing Dawn's suitcase from the back of his SUV. "Hey, want to go see what the dogs are doing?" Wade asked the boy, genuine delight visible in the man's brown eyes. Wade had always been good with little kids. With the exception of Calvin, Danny had never quite known what to say to them.

Of course, the dogs were already barking out their greetings at the front door from inside the house, so distracting Calvin away to go see them wasn't much of a challenge.

As Wade and the boy headed for the front door, Tanya stepped up to her sister beside the SUV. "You're taking him off to California? What are you thinking?"

"Not out here," Danny said, his gaze sweeping across the surrounding trees where anyone could be hiding, waiting for their chance to get at Dawn or Tanya. "Let's get moving."

As soon as they stepped inside, they could hear random happy dog barks and Calvin's laughter. It sounded like they were in the small den beyond the dining room. Maribel appeared from that direction to greet Dawn and ask if she was hungry or needed a cup of coffee.

"Coffee and snacks sound good to me," Danny said quickly. There was no telling how soon Calvin might return looking for his mom. "We'll meet you in the dining room in a few minutes."

Maribel nodded and headed back toward the kitchen.

Dawn turned to her sister. "I am so sorry for all that you've been through. I don't know how to express to you how thankful I am for how you protected Calvin."

Tanya, who'd appeared hardened with frustration until this moment, practically melted in front of Danny's eyes. The set of her shoulders softened, her mouth went slack and her hazel eyes filled with tears.

"I would do anything for Calvin," Tanya said softly. "I love him."

Danny wished he were in the kitchen with Maribel. Feeling like an intruder, he looked away from the women, first at his feet, then at the ceiling, next at the window and the river outside. Finally, he looked back at Tanya and Dawn. They weren't crying, exactly, but it was close. Danny's first impression when he'd seen Dawn was that the sisters didn't look at all alike. But for some reason, at this moment, they kind of did.

"I've been thinking about what's best for Calvin since you told me what happened," Dawn said to Tanya. "Getting him out of town seems like the best idea, and staying with Valerie and her husband seems like a good option."

"We can protect you and Calvin here," Danny said.

Dawn turned to him. "Valerie's husband is a marine. They live on the base at Camp Pendleton near San Diego." She glanced around. "This place looks secure, and based on what my sister has told me, I believe you know what you're doing. But all things considered, I think while you and local law enforcement track down whoever came after my boy and my sister, it will be best for Calvin and me to get out of town. I think a marine base is a very safe place for us to be."

Danny nodded. "I can't argue with that."

"Why is someone after you?" Tanya asked.

Her sister sighed heavily. "I really have no idea. I've wracked my brain about it. I sell real estate," she said with a quick glance at Danny. "I don't have any secret, special knowledge from that. I haven't sold a multimillion-dollar lair to some drug kingpin or anything like that. Just the usual stuff to normal people. I think these attackers have me confused with someone else."

"What about your ex-fiancé?" Danny asked.

"Elliott?" Dawn asked. She rolled her eyes and shook her head. "What about Elliott? He's the one who called off the wedding. I truly appreciate it now and realize that he did me a favor. Better to call off a wedding than get married when you know it's not something you truly want. He's a jerk, but he's no criminal."

"And Joe Flynn?" Danny prodded.

Dawn looked visibly taken aback. "What about Joe?" She shook her head. "You can't think he was involved in this. He wouldn't hurt Calvin. And he wouldn't hurt Tanya, either."

"Could he be involved in something illegal? Something that would put him in the crosshairs of a thug?"

"I don't think so."

Danny noted the hint of doubt in her voice.

"I don't know much about his private

life," she continued. "It's Calvin he's interested in having a relationship with, not me."

"Mom!" Calvin's voice carried from the dining room. "Can I have a cookie?"

"Who did you tell about your plans for California?" Danny asked quickly.

"Outside of my family and you, the only people I've talked to about it are Valerie and her husband."

"Mom!" Calvin hollered again.

Smiling beyond the concern in her eyes, Dawn started to walk toward her son's voice.

Danny exchanged glances with Tanya. Dawn and Calvin might actually be fine on a marine base in California, but he was still worried about Tanya's safety. She had seen someone she likely wasn't meant to see when she was kidnapped in the woods. Possibly the person who'd ordered the attacks. And that had Danny worried.

SEVEN

Tanya had always thought of Elliott Bridger's home as beautiful but not especially warm or inviting. It sat on a hillside facing a canyon with a tributary of the Range River meandering along at the bottom. There were other houses in the neighborhood that managed to look cozy and upscale at the same time, but from the road, Elliott's place presented itself as several panes of impersonal smoke-colored reflective glass.

"The view from the living room is breathtaking," Tanya said after directing Danny up the steep driveway that ran alongside the house and wrapped around to the main entrance located behind the house. She felt compelled to make some kind of positive comment because the thought that maybe she was being too hard on Elliott nagged at her. She'd been too quick to suspect him as she'd thought it over yesterday and last night. She'd voiced her concerns to Dawn when they'd taken her and Calvin back to the airport this morning, and Dawn had told her she was being ridiculous.

Maybe Dawn was right. Elliott had always been polite to Tanya. At the end of the day, if he'd realized he didn't want to spend the rest of his life with her sister, or that he wasn't willing to commit to being a father to Calvin, then breaking up with Dawn was the right thing to do. Although he could have done it sooner rather than waiting until they were so close to the wedding date.

"You've mentioned that Elliott is in the tech industry and that he moved here from Seattle to enjoy the beauty of the wilderness," Danny commented. "It looks like he's been pretty successful. What exactly does he do?"

"Good question. I know he's a programmer and he's developed some customized databases. He probably mentioned other things he's done, but I don't remember the specifics. Tech stuff isn't something I'm particularly interested in."

"Considering all the windows on this side of the house, I'd guess Elliott is watching us right now," Danny said as he steered his SUV closer to the residence.

"He's got security cameras, too," Tanya said, starting to feel a little nervous. Did Elliott have a reason to be concerned about his safety? Maybe her sister was wrong about her former fiancé. Maybe he wasn't such a harmless guy, after all.

"It's probably too much to ask that Victor and his thug friends are hiding out here and we'll have them locked up before the day is over," Danny said. "Of course, if Elliott is the mastermind behind the kidnappings, then our showing up here might rattle him enough that he'll send his hired goons out of town to evade capture and we'll find them that way. I'm sure the cops have already arranged it so they'll receive alerts if Victor uses his credit card or if his car's license plates get picked up by a reader once he gets on the interstate."

Tanya nodded, her gaze glued on the house and all that tinted glass as they drove by to reach the courtyard and the formal entrance.

Just showing up without calling first was a strategy Danny had insisted upon. He'd claimed that appearing unannounced could get them an unguarded, more truthful response from Elliott. He'd said that calling ahead of time would just give Elliott time to come up with a lie and polish it.

They got out of Danny's SUV and walked across the crushed gravel and up the steps to the wide covered porch.

Danny insisted on walking slightly in front, and Tanya didn't argue with him. While she'd never thought of Elliott as a particularly intimidating fellow, her stomach began tying itself in knots as she anticipated potentially coming face-to-face with the person who'd orchestrated the attacks on her and Calvin.

Rather than floor-to-ceiling glass, like there was on the street-facing side of the house, this side was standard construction with a couple of moderate-size clear glass windows. The door was made of heavy wood, and Danny stepped up to knock on it.

After a few moments, when there was no answer, he rang the doorbell. Still nothing. He moved closer and pressed his ear against the door.

"I don't hear anything," he said quietly. "Not even a TV."

"He usually has music playing," Tanya said.

Danny stepped back and glanced at the

windows. "I haven't noticed the curtains swaying or seen any shadows moving on the other side of them. Have you?"

Tanya shook her head. "No. I haven't noticed anything."

"I guess we didn't catch him at home."

"Should we call him?" Tanya asked.

"I hate to give him the advance warning, but we might have to. Since he works at home, it's not like we can go to his place of employment to try to find him and talk to him."

"Actually, we kind of can. He's part owner of a cooperative office in town. Maybe he's there."

"A cooperative office?"

"Yeah. He and a few of his friends in the business community rent space in town to use as a storefront office when they need to meet people. Plus, connectivity can be dicey when you get out into the canyons and some of the more remote locations, especially when the weather is rough. Sometimes relay equipment gets knocked out by high winds, ice or snow. So if one of them has problems like that, the office is a place where they can go to get connected and still have privacy, plus the use of printers, scanners and other peripherals if they need them. And during regular business hours, they have Kirby there to assist them."

"Kirby?"

"Kirby Heath. He works as an assistant for several of the co-op members, meaning he takes care of some of their online sales campaigns, company social media posts and that sort of thing," she explained as they got back to Danny's SUV.

"So how big is this office co-op?" Danny asked. "Do you know much about it?"

"I've been there a couple of times with Dawn and she's told me about it. It's not that big. Maybe twelve or fifteen members. But they can afford to keep Kirby there full-time. When he's not working on a specific project for somebody, he can do whatever he wants and still get paid. He can read, play an online game or do whatever."

"Sounds like a pretty good gig for someone who can stand to stay in an office all day."

Tanya cast him a sidelong glance. "Nothing wrong with being in an office."

Danny made the turn at the bottom of the driveway, and they followed the road down the hillside and back into the town of Range River.

"The office is on Indigo Street," Tanya said a couple of blocks ahead of the intersection where they'd need to turn.

"Of course it is," Danny said, his comment followed by a chuckle. "If you want to be cool and trendy, you wouldn't put your office any place else."

Indigo Street ran along the Range River, paralleling its north bank. You couldn't drive on the actual street. Back in the day, it had been paved with chunks of river stone and lumber and red brick to keep wagon wheels from sinking into the mud when it rained or the snow melted. A hundred years ago, Indigo Street was pretty much the town of Range River in its entirety. Now it was a pedestrian shopping mall.

Danny pulled into the municipal parking lot at the end of the historic street. He and Tanya climbed out of the SUV and headed to the old-style wooden sidewalk, making their way past the attractively weathered buildings.

This small tourist-magnet section of town housed shops where you could pay $300 for jeans that already had rips in them, restaurants with extensive vegan options and coffee shops with live music most evenings. At the very end of the road sat the beautiful old Still Waters Church.

"The co-op office is in the Gem State

Emporium building," Tanya said, gesturing toward the largest building. It was made of red brick and stood three stories tall. The bottom floor housed retail shops. The second and third floors were all offices.

As they walked, Danny kept an eye on who was around them. Tanya found herself doing the same thing. Since it was Friday, there were already a fair number of people milling around, and restaurants were setting up their outdoor seating for the lunchtime crowd.

There was a door at the corner of the emporium building. Danny opened it, and they faced a staircase and an elevator. They took the stairs to the third floor, and Tanya led the way down the carpeted hallway. At the midpoint, she stopped and reached for the handle on a door.

"Source Partners Group?" Danny said, reading the placard.

"Elliott said they had to pick a generic name so it would suit everyone."

She pushed open the door and smiled at the man seated at a desk in the lobby with three computer screens in front of him. Tanya knew he was in his midthirties, but she thought he looked much younger. He wore glasses with bright purple frames but was otherwise dressed completely in black. His short, spiky hair was heavily gelled and stood on end.

"Kirby, hi," Tanya called out in greeting.

"Hello, Tanya." Kirby got to his feet, smiling broadly.

Tanya thought she saw his smile falter.

"This is Danny Ryan," she added as the bounty hunter stepped up beside her. Beyond that, she wasn't quite sure how to proceed. If Elliott was here, should she just flat out ask him if he had ordered the attacks on her and Calvin?

While she stood frozen in indecision,

Danny moved past her and stepped up to Kirby's desk. "We'd like to speak with Elliott Bridger," he said.

"I'd like to speak to him, too," Kirby responded.

"He isn't here?" Tanya asked.

Kirby shifted his gaze to her and shook his head. "He was supposed to come by yesterday morning to discuss a lunch meeting he wanted me to arrange with some potential new clients, but he never showed up."

"Have you called him?" Danny asked.

Kirby sighed heavily. "I've texted, messaged and commented on his social media accounts. I haven't actually called him yet, because he doesn't like to talk on the phone."

"Did he make this appointment with you recently, like within the last day or two?" Danny asked.

"He put it on our shared work calendar about a month ago."

"Do you have any idea where he might be?" Tanya asked.

Kirby's expression turned cagey. "I was sorry to hear that things didn't work out between Elliott and your sister," he said. "Beyond that, I can only say that I don't get involved in my employers' private lives. So, no, I don't have any idea where he might be."

Tanya felt her cheeks flush with frustration. She didn't believe Kirby had no idea where Elliott was. She'd seen the friendly way Elliott and Kirby interacted on several occasions. They chatted about gaming, new tech equipment about to hit the market and upcoming phone updates. They were friends. She was getting the impression that Kirby thought her and Danny's appearance here was related to some kind of relationship drama. Maybe that was why he was lying.

She shot a questioning glance in Danny's direction. Should she explain to

Kirby why they were looking for Elliott? The news reports about the initial kidnapping attempt had left out all identifying information since Calvin was a child. The attack on Tanya outside her aunt's home had not made it into the news beyond a generic mention in the local paper. Detective Romanov had made sure the information shared with the press had been bland in order to protect Tanya and Calvin as well as the ongoing investigation. So there was no reason for Kirby to know why Tanya and Danny were here. It was certainly possible that the police had come by here looking for Elliott and spoken to Kirby about the kidnapping attempt, but maybe they hadn't yet.

Danny returned her glance and shook his head slightly. She took that as an indication he didn't want her to give away too much information. "I guess we'll just have to catch up with Elliott later," Danny said to Kirby. "It was good to meet you."

"Likewise," Kirby said pleasantly.

Disappointed, Tanya forced a smile on her lips. "Thanks, Kirby. See you later."

As they strode down the hallway to the exit, Danny turned to her. "We can assume Kirby will let Elliott know we were here, so you might as well call Elliott. Or text him, I guess. Maybe both."

"He's going to think it's weird if he hears from me. If he is behind the attacks, it might tip our hand that we suspect him, because there's really no other reason for me to be calling him."

"Good point. Can you think of any reason why you'd want to talk to him that wouldn't make him suspicious?"

"Maybe something work-related." She thought for a minute. When they got to the bottom of the stairs, she stopped and dug her phone out of her purse. "Elliott and I talked a couple of times about me wanting to open my own accounting business someday, and how I'd need tech help when I did. I'm going to leave a message telling him that I've decided to go ahead with it and I need help with the website. Either from him or somebody he can recommend. If he actually answers, I'll ask if we can meet to discuss website designs."

"And that won't make him suspicious? You and he were on good terms after he broke things off with your sister?"

"What I thought about him after he broke up with Dawn wouldn't necessarily be described as good, but I never actually saw him after the breakup, so he has no idea how I felt."

She hadn't gotten around to deleting Elliott's number from her phone, so she was able to find it in the directory and tap the icon. As expected, it went to voice mail. She left her message and followed it with a text in case that might get a quicker response.

The walk along Indigo Street back to

the SUV had them breathing in the scents of mouthwatering food.

"I'm hungry," Tanya said when the smell of bratwurst cooking on an outdoor grill became too hard to resist. "You want to stop and get something? Do you think it would be safe to do that?"

"Sure," Danny said. "As long as we eat inside."

"Right." Because she might still be a target after what she'd seen and overheard in the forest. Even though those memories were a little scrambled, the bad guys couldn't know that, or that she didn't really get a good look at the third man who was there.

Shaking off the horrible memory of those moments of being held captive in the forest, she realized Danny had just asked her where she wanted to eat. She gestured at the Bavarian Haus.

"Looks and smells good to me," Danny said.

They headed inside.

"Maybe you'll hear from Elliott while we're eating," he added after they were seated. "If not, after we're done, let's see if we can track down somebody else to talk to."

After lunch they continued their investigation.

"I didn't spend much time around Dawn and Joe back when they were a couple," Tanya said. They were on the road in the SUV, and Danny had just made the turn she'd indicated. "So I can't tell you much about him."

At the end of lunch, Danny had suggested that they try to question Joe Flynn, and Tanya had readily agreed. Now, Danny was trying to decide if having Tanya with him when he approached Joe would help or hurt his chances at getting any useful information out of the man. It was pretty clear Tanya still resented Calvin's father for offering no emotional support when Dawn found out she was pregnant.

"I know that Joe owns the auto body repair shop we're headed to, Champion Auto Body," she added. "Supposedly he's a hard worker, and Dawn has never complained about him not paying child support." There was a thoughtful silence before she added, "I don't know what his problem was back when Dawn really needed him. I've approached the issue with her a few times, but she's made it clear she doesn't want to talk about it. Or him. Not with me, anyway."

Danny further considered the strategy he wanted to use when he questioned Joe. Yesterday, after they'd picked up Dawn at the airport, Detective Romanov had come by the inn to interview her. The cop had expressed her intent to interview Elliott and Joe, as well. Maybe she already had. That might be why Elliott was now hard to find. He could be aware that he was a suspect. It could also mean that Joe knew about the attack on Tanya and his son. He might be angry at Tanya for not telling him about it.

Champion Auto Body was a moderate-size shop with six work bays and a small but tidy front office. A window spanned the wall behind the service counter, and through it, Danny could see several expensive cars and trucks being worked on. Joe clearly catered to some high-end clients.

"Good afternoon. How can we help you?" A young man with the name Robbie stitched onto his shirtfront walked up to the counter to greet them.

"We're here to talk to Joe," Tanya said.

Danny held back a grimace at the sharp tone in her voice. Robbie, who was clearly skilled at customer service, didn't indicate that he'd noticed it. "Is he expecting you?" he asked pleasantly.

"No, but I'm his son's aunt. He should want to talk to me."

"Tanya."

Danny turned toward the voice. A man had stepped out of an office, and he looked a lot like Calvin. Same brown hair, same brown eyes. A similar shape to his face. But while Calvin's expression was generally sweet and trusting—except for moments when the poor little guy was thinking about the attacks on him—this man's expression was hard and suspicious.

"Joe," Tanya said, taking a few steps toward him. "Do you have a few minutes to talk?"

"About what?" He crossed his arms over his chest. His gaze flickered from Tanya to Danny and then back again.

"I need to talk to you about Calvin. And Dawn." Her voice fractured, and she cleared her throat. "Something happened."

"You want to talk to me about it *now*? *Three days* after it happened?"

"I thought it was Dawn's place to decide when and how to tell you."

"She didn't inform me. I found out about it when the police came by my home to question me the day after the thugs tried to kidnap my boy."

Danny couldn't say for certain, but it looked like the glittering hardness in the man's eyes had shifted to an expression of pain.

Joe wiped his hand across his face, turned and stepped back into his office. Tanya followed him, and Danny followed her.

"Who are you?" Joe said to Danny from behind his desk.

"My name is Danny Ryan, and I'm a bounty hunter."

"A bounty hunter?" Joe's eyebrows lifted slightly.

"One of the assailants is a bail jumper

that I'm tracking. How do you know Victor Durbin?"

Joe frowned. "The detective who questioned me brought up the same name. Like I told her, I don't know him."

Maybe he was telling the truth. Maybe he wasn't. Maybe he knew Victor under a different name. "Did she show you a picture of him?" Danny asked.

"No."

Danny grabbed his phone from his pocket, pulled up the photo of Victor and handed it over. "Take a good look. Have you seen him around?"

Joe looked at it and nodded slightly to himself. Then he handed the phone back to Danny. "No. Never seen him in my life. You're saying this is the piece of garbage who came after my boy?" He glanced at Tanya. "And came after you?"

Danny slid a business card out of his wallet and set it on Joe's desk. Unless Joe was faking his responses, Danny had a pretty good idea what was going on in the guy's mind. "If you think you see him, call the cops or call me. *Listen to me.* You'll want to see him face due process and get locked up for a long time. You don't want to end up in prison yourself where you'll be kept away from your son. So don't take things into your own hands."

Joe stared at him without responding. He didn't even reach for the card.

Danny placed a finger on the card and slid it a little closer toward him. He hoped that when and if the time came and Joe actually did spot Victor somewhere in town, that he would keep a cool head and do the right thing. Of course, the possibility that Joe was somehow involved in the attacks still existed.

Joe turned to Tanya. "Are you here because you really think I'd be involved in something that could put my son in danger? Or put you in danger? Do you really think that little of me?"

"I don't know what to think," she responded warily.

Joe took in a deep breath and blew it out. "You're suspicious of me because I'm trying to get my custody rights revisited. That's it, isn't it? You don't like me, I know that. And you don't want me to have access to my son."

Tanya crossed her arms over her chest, mirroring his defensive body language. "You weren't there for Calvin and Dawn when they needed you the most."

Danny figured this was probably a good time for them to leave, before things between Tanya and Joe got any more heated. He quickly said goodbye to Joe, prompted Tanya to do the same, and they left.

"You didn't mention anything about a revisited custody agreement between Joe and Dawn," Danny said once they were outside.

Tanya shook her head. "I didn't know about it. That's something new."

"It's significant. People sometimes do emotionally charged, irrational things when it comes to their kids. Maybe Joe had something to do with the abduction. Maybe he hired Victor and Max. Maybe they weren't authorized to use deadly force around Calvin but things got out of control. It could be that they tried to grab you after that because they'd failed in their first attempt and were trying to salvage the mission."

"I suppose that might be what happened," Tanya said, exhaling loudly.

"Could Joe have been the unidentified man you saw in the woods?"

"I don't know. I didn't get a good look. I had the impression that the guy had some money. Joe is looking pretty prosperous these days. I guess it's possible it was him." She shook her head. "There are so many bits of information about what's happened over the last few days swirling around in my head, but I can't get them to fit into any kind of pattern."

"There's always a period of time like that in an investigation," Danny said as they got into the SUV. "Eventually, things start to fit together."

"Yeah, well, I don't like to wait. I like things to fit together quickly." She sat up straighter. "Let's go by my office. Helen's probably still there. I want to talk to her about me maybe doing some work while I'm off over the next few days."

"Don't you want to take a break from everything? Haven't you been under enough stress?"

"I've had enough stress, yes. But I'm hoping I can arrange for her to send me some basic tasks or simple audits to do while I'm away from work. Something where I can line up everything, get it organized and have it all make sense. It would be an actual de-stressor for me.

I'd rather do that during my downtime or when I can't sleep rather than just sit and worry."

"Okay."

They headed for Tanya's office. When they reached their destination, Danny parked in the small lot beside the business complex. They had just gotten out of the SUV when someone fired a shot at them.

EIGHT

Five more gunshots followed the first, and a car careened around the corner, turning from the main street onto the smaller road running alongside the parking lot.

Tanya dived to the ground and scrambled to get underneath the SUV, feeling the burn from losing a strip of skin on her chin when she scraped it on the asphalt. Danny crouched down beside his vehicle. He didn't take cover underneath it alongside her. Instead, he used the SUV as a barricade.

Tanya turned her head, unable to see much more than the scattered fragments of glass on the pavement. The sound of the car involved in the attack faded away.

Adrenaline sent her body shaking, and her unsteady emotions seemed to match the physical movements. Despair threatened to overwhelm her. These attacks were relentless. It seemed like they were never going to end.

Using small movements in the restricted space beneath the SUV, she turned toward Danny. She saw his booted feet on the pavement. Then she saw something else close beside his feet. Drops of blood. Her hammering heart felt like it suddenly stopped.

Danny's been shot.

"You're hurt!" she called out, barely able to hear her own voice over the spiral-sounding car alarms and honking horns that had been triggered by the gunfire. A crushing sense of guilt threatened to pin her in place as she realized that Danny had been out there facing danger while she'd been hiding under the SUV.

"It's nothing," he answered back.

Of course he would say that.

She began to scoot out from beneath the vehicle to see for herself if he was okay. He could need help. Maybe he needed her to put pressure on a gunshot wound to keep him alive. He might need an ambulance. With all the car alarms going off and the sounds of gunshots, somebody in the office complex must have called 9-1-1. The dispatcher would send emergency medical services to respond along with the cops, right?

What if Danny had injuries that required immediate first aid? She didn't know what to do. She needed her phone. It was in her purse. Where was her purse? She must have dropped it when the shooting started.

She clambered out from beneath the SUV and saw Danny, still crouching, with his face turned away. He held a gun in his right hand and pressed his left hand to his collarbone near the base of his neck.

He turned toward her, and she saw that blood had seeped down onto the front of his shirt.

"You're hurt," she said again before crawling toward him. "Let me take a look."

"A small cut. Looks worse than it is. A chunk of glass or plastic from a mirror must have hit me."

"How do you know it didn't hit an artery?"

He let go of a grim laugh. "If it had, I'd be unconscious by now."

Oh, yeah. If she weren't freaking out, she would have thought of that.

"Where are the cops?" she said. "They're taking forever to get here."

"It always feels like forever when your life is in danger."

A second-story window on the back of the office building slid partway open. "Hey!" a male voice called out. "Are you okay? What happened?"

"Call the police!" Danny yelled.

"Already done," the voice responded.

"Can you open up your back door and let us into the building?" Tanya called out.

There was no response. The window slammed shut.

"He's probably scared," Danny said. "He doesn't know what's going on. Doesn't know who the good guys are and who the bad guys are. Happens a lot with bystanders."

"You think the shooters are gone?" Tanya asked. "Can we stand up?" What she wanted to do was get Danny out of the chilly air, get him water and have him sit down and rest. She still hadn't seen his wound. It could be worse than he thought.

"Stay down," Danny said. "I'm going to stand up and take a quick look. Make sure the bad guys aren't lurking round here somewhere."

Tanya's gaze settled on the gun in his hand as he slowly stood. She hadn't heard him return fire during the event. There were occupied buildings on the other side of the street. People could have gotten hit by a stray bullet. He'd been careful and controlled, and she was glad of that.

One by one, the car alarms stopped. They hadn't blared long enough to run down the car batteries, so people inside the office building must have turned them off. Nevertheless, no one stepped outside.

Tanya heard the wail of sirens. Help was almost here. *Finally.*

"Move your hand away from your neck and let me see your injury," she said to Danny.

He grinned. "Why? Are you worried about me?"

She rolled her eyes. Then she heard the crack of gunfire followed by the *plink* of metal striking metal. A bullet tore a hole in the car to her right, barely missing her. She heard a second shot, followed by the metallic *plink* sound as she and Danny dived back toward the asphalt.

Then she heard the growl of an engine as a car accelerated. The gunmen must have circled back after they initially sped away. The shooter must have gotten out of the car and sneaked up to the parking lot on foot.

The criminals' determination was fierce, and there was no denying that Tanya was now their target.

"Whenever you get hungry, let me know," Maribel said to Tanya. "I'll be happy to fix you something to eat."

"Thank you." Tanya lifted the mug full of hot cocoa she was holding. "This is fine right now." She took a sip of the creamy drink and felt her tense muscles relax a little as she savored the sweet, chocolaty taste.

She was seated in a wingback chair in the first-floor office at the Riverside Inn.

All three members of the Ryan family, plus Wade, were seated on the chairs and sofa in the room, which was set up more like a den than a standard office.

Maribel picked up an electronic tablet from the heavy, antique oak desk that dominated the room and then lowered herself into the thickly padded swivel chair behind it. She tapped the screen a few times, apparently prepping to take notes, and then gave Connor a slight nod.

The leader of the Range River bounty hunters turned to Tanya. "How are you feeling?"

"I'm fine," she said, surprised to hear herself sounding defensive. She was also surprised to feel tears well up in the corners of her eyes and a knot in the center of her chest. It was like the fear and horror from the last few days had been shoved down, but she couldn't hold them there much longer. Especially not if she kept talking.

The shooting in the parking lot had happened three hours ago. Enough time had passed for law enforcement to arrive, for the ambulance to show up, and for Tanya to reassure Helen that she was okay. Her boss had made her way out to the parking lot once the police were there and it was clear the situation was stabilized.

Tanya had been interviewed by Detective Romanov, who'd arrived on the scene looking stony-faced and who'd been focused on making a big-picture assessment of the situation, looking for security cameras and trying to find potential witnesses in the surrounding businesses before people went home for the day.

All those things and more had happened since that car sped by firing shots and then the gunman had returned on foot to try and finish her off. So why did it feel like she'd dived under that vehicle and scraped her chin just moments ago? Why was it that when she closed her eyes, she felt like all the horrible events were still happening right now? Was she losing it?

Tanya shook her head, tired of feeling like she was stuck in some weird loop, wanting to shake herself free from the mental trap. She turned to Danny, who was seated in the chair closest to her. "Everyone should be asking how *you* are doing," she said, her gaze settling on the patch of cotton bandage visible at the collar of his clean shirt. The paramedic had confirmed that Danny had sustained a pretty good cut near his collarbone, but that the injury was not life-threatening.

If the bit of flying debris had hit him an inch or so higher, it would have struck his carotid artery and things would have ended much differently. Danny likely wouldn't have survived. *Thank You, Lord*, Tanya prayed, for what felt like the hundredth time today. She was so grateful with every fiber of her being that she would happily pray it another hundred times.

"I'm fine," Danny told her. "I'm sure this cut doesn't hurt nearly as much as that scrape on your chin does. Those things burn."

Yeah, Danny probably was fine.

Tanya wasn't.

All these people around her in this room seemed all right despite what had happened. Maybe they hadn't been shot at today, but someone they loved had. Danny could have been killed. While there'd been lots of hugs and concerned inquiries when the Range River Bail Bonds crew showed up at the scene, they'd seemed to have gotten over it pretty quickly. They'd eaten a hearty dinner while Tanya sat at the table, barely able to sip water.

She appreciated the help these people were offering her more than she could say, but she was not like them. She needed order in her life. She needed predictability. She needed to understand what was happening. And even if she weren't in danger herself, she couldn't possibly live with someone she loved being in danger on a regular basis.

She took another sip of cocoa and stole a glance at Danny. He wore the genial expression he normally did, but now it looked like a mask to her. Not that he was hiding who he truly was, but she could see the tension underneath the easygoing exterior. The controlled anger at what had happened today, and the determination to do something about it.

When she'd first realized who the bounty hunter was after the attempted abduction of Calvin, she'd assumed she knew Danny Ryan fairly well. That he might be nice, and he was admittedly handsome, but she'd thought there was nothing solid beneath that. No depth of character. Now she knew better.

She also knew better than to let herself develop any serious feelings for him. After spending three days together, he'd started to feel like a friend. If she were honest with herself, he was maybe someone who could be more than a friend. But she knew now that she had to make that feeling stop dead in its tracks, because the kind of life that he lived as a bounty hunter was not a life she could share with him. There was no way.

"So what are we going to do next?" Connor asked Danny. "What's the plan?"

They had not talked about the parking lot shooting during dinner. After Hayley had said grace over the meal, the conversation had been light and low-key. Tanya suspected that might have been for her benefit, because she was obviously still upset. But now they clearly wanted to get down to business.

"The next step, after a good night's sleep, will be to go to the police station tomorrow morning to talk to Detective Romanov," Danny responded.

"Tomorrow is Saturday," Maribel interjected.

"I know. She asked if we'd mind coming in, and we told her we'd be okay with it." He glanced over at Tanya, and she nodded in agreement. "Along with answering questions and seeing if we can come up with any more pertinent memories of what happened today, she's got some more mug shots for us to look at to see if we can identify the third man Tanya saw talking to Victor and Max when they grabbed her in the forest."

Tanya sighed. She hadn't gotten a look at that guy's face. She didn't have any more useful information to offer.

"What can we do to help you guys?" Wade asked. "Do you have any leads we can track down? Anybody we can interview for you?"

"Use your informants," Danny said.

"Ask them about Victor and Max. About Elliott and Joe. See if they know anything."

"You think today's attack is connected to your conversation with Joe Flynn?" Hayley asked. "The timing points to it. You two had just talked to him."

"Yeah, but we tried to talk to Elliott, too," Tanya said. "And he seems to be trying really hard to stay out of sight. I'm sure his assistant, Kirby, called him as soon as we left the co-op office."

"But what would Elliott's motive be?" Hayley asked.

Tanya shook her head. "I don't know."

"All right," Connor said, getting to his feet. "Hayley, Wade and I will start pushing our informants for intel on our bail jumpers plus the other suspected bad guys. Danny and Tanya will talk to the cops and look at mug shots. We'll see what kind of information we can turn up and go from there."

Danny turned to Tanya. "Don't worry, we'll keep moving forward on this. We won't quit until you're safe."

His earnestness pulled at her heart. It ached a little to know things couldn't work out between the two of them, because she really did like him.

"Thank you," she said crisply, determined to strengthen her resolve to hold back emotionally and keep things businesslike. She sighed heavily. "I think I'm going to turn in early. But first I think I'll give Dawn a quick call and make sure she and Calvin are okay."

She got to her feet. Maybe tomorrow she'd feel stronger. The only way to make it through dark times was to lean into her faith and keep pushing forward. It was hard, but she would do it. She had to, along with the cops and the bounty hunters who were refusing to quit, too. Because the bad guys weren't going to stop on their own, and she and Dawn and

Calvin deserved to have their peaceful, normal lives back.

"You really hate me, don't you?" Joe kept the volume of his voice low as he spat the words to Tanya in the lobby of the police department.

He was on his way out while Danny and Tanya were arriving early for their appointment with Detective Romanov.

"I can't believe you're trying to get the police to believe I would somehow be behind an attack on my own son."

His words might not be loud, but his intense anger and frustration were evident in the expression on his face and in his squared shoulders and fisted hands. Afraid that he might snap and strike out at Tanya, Danny stepped forward to put himself between them.

To Danny's surprise, Tanya stepped around him.

"Are you involved?" she demanded of

Joe. "Did you hire those thugs to come after Calvin and me? Did you shoot at us—or have somebody shoot at us—yesterday after we talked to you at your shop and made you mad?"

Joe took a couple of aimless steps, shoving up his shirtsleeves and looking like he wanted to punch something. Maybe a nearby wall. Or perhaps even Tanya. If the guy was a hothead with impulse-control issues, being at the police department wasn't going to stop him from acting out.

Tanya didn't have the life experience Danny had reading body language, and she probably didn't realize the volatility of the situation. The bounty hunter was about to reach out and once again put himself between Tanya and Joe when Joe took in a deep breath, blew it out and unclenched his fists.

Joe's tensed-up shoulders dropped down, and he tilted his head slightly. "I'm not involved in any of this. But because people are determined to think the worst of me, I can't see my son. Dawn won't take my calls. I'm not even sure where my boy is right now."

"You abandoned him before he was even born and didn't have anything to do with him until he was four years old. Yeah, you sent money. That was nice of you."

The way she emphasized the word *nice* made it clear to Danny—and from the expression on Joe's face, it must have been clear to him, too—that she meant it sarcastically.

"Doing what you're legally obligated to do doesn't exactly make you father of the year," she added.

"You're right, it doesn't," Joe said. "But haven't you ever done something you later regretted?"

Tanya crossed her arms over her chest. "I never abandoned a child."

Joe held her gaze for a moment, then

nodded and walked past her and Danny and out the police department door.

"Let me go over and talk to the desk sergeant to see if Detective Romanov is ready to speak with us." Danny turned and walked toward the reception counter, realizing the uniformed cop standing on the other side had been observing their conversation. Within a couple of minutes, the sergeant was ushering them to Detective Romanov's office.

"You think Joe's involved?" Tanya asked as soon as they were seated in the detective's office.

Romanov shrugged noncommittally. "I'm still at the stage where I'm adding suspects to my list. I'm not taking any off. Not yet. We're researching backgrounds, checking alibis, working out timelines for who was where at what time. All that takes longer than most people realize."

Danny decided that researching Joe was going to be the top priority for him and the Range River team. That guy seemed primed to explode. He had a pretty big chip on his shoulder. A motive wasn't clear. If he really wanted more time with his son, and if Dawn was fighting him on that point and he was angry, that could be a motive. An irrational one, but people did sometimes get caught up in intense emotions and do things that worked against them. Maybe this was just a guy who figured he should always get what he wanted when he wanted it. Maybe he held a grudge against Dawn and Tanya and he simply wanted to torment them. Maybe he'd hired the assailants to do just that. Or maybe he'd hired the guy Tanya saw in the woods, and that man had hired the assailants.

"Take your time looking at these photos," Detective Romanov said, handing over a tablet. "Hopefully one will be the mystery guy in the woods."

Tanya began swiping the screen of the

tablet, looking at an array of men whose commonality appeared to be that they were in their thirties or forties and that they were slender and dark-haired.

"Who are these guys?" Tanya asked, her gaze still focused on the screen.

"Maybe they're connected to the attack on you," the detective said. "You tell me."

Tanya blew out a sigh of frustration and looked up at Romanov, shaking her head. "I told you, I told everybody, I didn't get a clear look at the man's face. I'd been hit in the head. I was dizzy and groggy when I saw him."

"I'm not trying to put pressure on you to identify someone if you can't," Romanov said. "But maybe one of them looks familiar."

"These are men known to have been involved in crimes like the attempted kidnapping of Tanya in the woods?" Danny asked.

Tanya looked up. "There are this many kidnappers in Range River?"

Romanov shook her head. "No, these are culled from people who have been charged with kidnapping in the state of Idaho at some point over the last twenty years."

Tanya made her way through the pictures before returning the tablet to the detective. "I just had an impression of a slender man with dark hair. I don't remember any details about how he looked. I'm sorry."

"No need to apologize."

"I heard his voice while they were talking about tech stuff."

"Tech stuff?" Danny said, turning to her. "You never mentioned them talking about tech stuff before. You said you heard them talking but you couldn't really make sense of what they were saying."

"Well, I guess I didn't remember it until now." Tanya sounded apologetic.

"You've experienced a lot of trauma in a short amount of time," Romanov said. "That's not something a person just bounces back from. Remembering further details as time passes is common. It's one of the reasons why we ask people to come back in and recount what happened again."

Tanya nodded. "So, tech stuff. That means this could be connected to Elliott."

"Or not," Romanov said. "That's a pretty common topic of conversation. What exactly did you hear them say?"

"Oh, something about everything being debugged and ready for rollout. Something being configured, maybe."

"What was being debugged and ready for rollout?" Romanov asked.

"I don't know. I mean, I just remember a jumble of words, and those were some of them."

"Those are actually pretty general terms," Danny said. "People could use them for all kinds of situations and applications, not just technology-based ones."

Tanya shrugged. "You're right. Maybe I'm just trying to force it into making sense with what I know, tying it to Elliott just because he's familiar."

Tanya closed her eyes and rubbed her temples. It looked like she had a headache. Danny's attention was drawn to the bandage on her chin, where the skin had been scraped off by the asphalt. Maybe it was a small injury, but it was also a visual reminder of how much the woman had been through in just a few days. Physically and emotionally.

"Now that I think about it, he might not have been talking to Victor and Max," Tanya said. "I think he was farther down the hill. He was pacing when he was talking. He might have been on a phone."

"Yesterday afternoon, you mentioned attempts to contact Elliott and your visit with Joe," the detective said, shifting her gaze between Tanya and Danny. "I was a little too busy at the scene to follow up. How about you two fill me in on exactly how all that went?"

Tanya gestured at Danny, indicating that she wanted him to do most of the talking. So he did. Tanya jumped in occasionally to add a few details. When their recitation was finished, Danny locked eyes with Detective Romanov. "Now, what have you got that you can share with us?"

In times past, the detective hadn't shared much of anything with him on cases he was working. He was expecting more of the same, especially when she stared at him and took a long time to respond. But finally, she leaned back into a more relaxed posture.

"We're actively looking for Victor and Max, and we've got enough for warrants to look at cell and credit card use. So far, those are dormant, so they probably have new phones and are using cash. As far as Joe or Elliott are concerned, we don't have enough evidence yet on either of them to get warrants for deep research on banking history or phone records or even credit card transactions. Which is aggravating. I'm hoping last night's shooting got picked up on some business security cameras in the neighborhood. We don't have many traffic surveillance cameras like the larger towns and cities do."

"What about the bullets left behind last night, plus the evidence from when Max shot at me outside my house?" Tanya asked.

"That could help us get a conviction down the road if we have a suspect with a gun that's a ballistic match, but right now that evidence isn't helping us find the shooter or shooters."

The detective stood, signaling the end of the interview. Moments later, Danny walked outside beside Tanya, feeling like the wheels of police work were moving at an agonizingly slow rate. That worried him, because the attacks on Tanya were becoming much more brazen. Everyone working on this case wanted to catch the bad guys before they got to Tanya, but it was starting to look like they were running out of time.

NINE

Whatsoever things are lovely, whatsoever things are of good report...think on these things.

Tanya had gone to services at Still Waters Church with the bounty hunters earlier in the morning, and the words from the pastor's Sunday sermon still lingered in her mind. This was not the first time she'd needed to use a Bible verse to anchor her emotions and get her thoughts going in the right direction.

Events from the last few days kept playing through her mind, with the most recent shooting being the most vivid. Three times last night, she'd woken from gunshots in her nightmares, the sounds so loud and seemingly so real that she'd had the sensation of ringing in her ears for a few seconds after she first opened her eyes.

"It's funny how watching the river flowing by can be so calming," Danny said. He'd just opened the slider door from the inn's great room and stepped out onto the deck where Tanya was sitting in a low-slung chair with a hand-knitted throw across her lap. Danny handed her a mug of coffee and then turned to close the door behind him before walking farther out onto the deck.

Tanya had placed her chair beside a row of potted evergreen shrubs that Maribel had pointed out could be used as a wind-break if needed. Or a privacy screen when there were a lot of people floating by on the river in the summer.

Right now, Tanya was using the thick foliage to help her stay hidden and avoid being shot by a sniper. Because that was

her life now. Trying not to get herself—
or someone else—killed. She was determined to be careful and mindful, but she
could not completely lock herself up inside the inn and cower in fear. Not if she
wanted to hang on to her sanity. It was
Hayley who had convinced her to get out
and go to church this morning. It was also
Hayley who had pointed out that it was
possible to feel fear, and to be attentive to
what it was signaling to you without being
completely overwhelmed by it.

Tanya stole a quick look at Danny. He
stood sipping his afternoon coffee and
gazing at the water flowing by just beyond the railing. The large white bandage
was gone from his collar area. He had a
smaller, less noticeable adhesive patch in
its place now. That felt like confirmation
that his injury was not terribly serious.
Still, she knew it had to hurt.

He glanced over at her. "Mind if I sit out
here with you?"

"Of course not."

He pulled over a chair and dropped down into it. He'd cleaned up nicely for church this morning, including a splash of aftershave with a hint of cedar. She could smell it now as he sat beside her. There was something comforting and appealing about it.

He wore the same thoughtful expression on his face that he'd had in church. There was no denying that he'd changed a lot since they were teenagers. Hopefully, everyone developed to some degree. The thought led Tanya to wonder about herself.

With her parents constantly splitting up and getting back together until her dad finally moved out for good, all she'd ever wanted was stability and order. Now she had to wonder if she'd held on to that desire too tightly and for too long. Because what was happening in her life right now was certainly proving that trusting the

Lord and being able to adapt on the fly might be the more realistic and worthwhile goal.

Danny quietly drank his coffee and took in the beautiful scenery. After spending a few moments watching him, Tanya realized his head was moving slowly and slightly from side to side. He was scanning their surroundings.

"Is being vigilant a conscious decision for you?" she asked. "Or does it just go with your mildly hyper personality?"

Danny laughed, stretching out his long legs and crossing his booted feet at the ankles. "I suppose it's a little of both."

Tanya turned away to look in the direction the river was flowing, westward, toward the Pacific Ocean. The sun had already dropped low in the sky. Shadows spilled down the sides of the nearby mountaintops, pooling in the ridgelines. Those shadows would eventually reach the town of Range River, where they could hide anything or anyone, including the people who wanted Tanya dead.

"Why are those thugs so intent on killing me?" she asked Danny. She didn't really expect him to have the answer. But it was nice to feel companionship while she mulled over such a lonely question.

"Well, since you weren't the target originally, my guess is that now it's because of who you saw or what you heard in the forest outside your aunt's house. Or what they believe you heard, I should say."

"Perhaps the most recent attack happened because I've been out and about with you asking questions and stirring things up. But if that were the case, why wouldn't they come after you, too?"

Danny waited several seconds before he answered. "They kind of did," he said quietly.

She turned to him and let her eyes drop to his collar, to his injury, and she couldn't help feeling responsible for the fact that he'd been hurt. Tears of anger and frustration began to form in the corners of her eyes. It felt like she'd been fighting them all day despite leaning into the strengthening Bible verse that had caught her attention this morning.

Exhaustion was wearing her down. She wanted to go home. What she wanted most of all was to know that Dawn and Calvin were safe and sound and would remain that way. Though it seemed petty in the context of all that was happening, she really missed her normal routine. It felt like forever since she'd been able to stop at her favorite coffee stand in the morning, or get a cheeseburger and chocolate shake for lunch from her favorite café near the office.

"I'm sorry," Tanya said, impatiently brushing away a tear. "I'm being self-centered. I know better."

"Fear can do that to a person," Danny

said easily. "No need to apologize. Happens to everybody."

"Not to you. You look out for other people."

"So do you. Come on, running out of the house with a baseball bat to rescue Calvin?" He grinned and shook his head. "That's an image I'll never forget."

She found herself laughing and crying, and a little bit of her pent-up tension seemed to lift off her chest and drift away.

"It's easier for me to cope with what's been happening because I'm not the bad guys' prime target," he said, the smile on his face fading away. "I'm just the guy helping you while searching for my bail jumper. They shot at me because I got in their way."

"They wouldn't dare target you, anyway," Tanya said. "You've got a whole family full of bounty hunters looking out for you."

"My bounty-hunter family is looking out for you, too."

He was right. And the pastor's sermon this morning had been right. Much as she wasn't naturally inclined at the moment to think on all the good things in her life, that was exactly what she needed to do.

"I keep thinking about that mystery man in the forest," she said.

"Have you remembered something new?" Danny asked, sitting up straighter, fixing his intent gaze on her.

"Not really. At the time I saw him, I was woozy from getting hit on the head. And dizzy. My thoughts were focused more on where I was, what was happening, where they were standing and how I could get away from them. Not so much on him." A moment later, she laughed softly.

Danny quirked an eyebrow.

"I just realized that even in the midst of it all, I was being my accountant self," she said to explain her laughter. "I was trying to organize things. Put them into a pattern so I could deal with them."

"Nothing wrong with that," Danny said. "Everybody's got their quirks. To me, being an accountant and wanting things to be all nice and orderly all the time is kind of odd. I like an unexpected challenge. I'm good at improvising. Being odd doesn't mean you're wrong. Even if what you do or how you behave sometimes annoys other people."

"Why do I get the feeling somebody said that to you? Gave you a pep talk about it being okay even if you're kind of different?"

Danny grinned. "That's exactly what happened when I was in middle school and kept getting into trouble because I just couldn't sit still. Connor dragged me to a counselor recommended by our pastor. When she told me God loves and can use all kinds of people exactly as they are, I can't tell you what that did for me. I had her repeat what she'd told me to Connor. After that, the counselor and I worked on things I could do to stop making my teachers want to pull their hair out."

"And now some of those same traits that were a problem back then help you to do your job as a bounty hunter. Like being hyperaware of your surroundings or reacting quickly to a change in your environment."

He nodded. "I did naturally mellow out a little as I aged. But still, it's funny how things develop over time. The characteristics that didn't appear to be blessings in the beginning eventually turned out to be just that." He took another sip of coffee. "So you said you've been thinking about the mystery man in the woods."

"I was just pondering how it's true that the technology-related terms he used are common for all kinds of conversations. They've moved from the tech realm to the general realm. Still, it seems like too much of a coincidence. Elliott broke off the engagement with my sister, the attacks started and now Elliott has made himself scarce. I believe the man in the forest could have been talking to Elliott, and I think we should focus on finding him."

"Elliott's definitely a person I want to talk to. But we don't have enough information to narrow our focus on any single person yet. It's still too early to organize what we know into a pattern and commit to a theory. We've got to keep things more open-ended."

"I hate that," Tanya muttered.

"I know." Danny nodded. "But trying to wrap things up too quickly before you have the necessary facts can be deadly."

Tanya shivered. Partly from the chill in the air, but also from fear. She wondered if she might have seen or heard something important in recent days but hadn't recognized it as a threat because it didn't fit into a predictable pattern. That meant she might not be able to escape the trouble that was coming.

"If at any time you change your mind and start to feel anxious, let me know, and I'll take you back to the inn," Danny said to Tanya as he made a turn off a road in downtown Range River and pulled into the parking lot of a shopping center with a grocery store and several other businesses.

"I'll be fine," she responded. "And if I need a break, I'd really like to go visit Aunt Winnie. Or go home. I want to do something that feels normal."

Danny glanced over at her and saw her smiling ruefully and shaking her head. "I know my coworkers are not going to want to see me back at the office for a while," she added. "Not after I caused a shoot-out in the parking lot."

"The shooting was not your fault," Danny said, threading his SUV through the parking lot and toward the Range River Bail Bonds office. "Don't ever put the blame for someone else's bad or violent behavior on yourself."

"Right," she said, not sounding completely convinced.

"And you know your boss isn't holding a grudge. She sent you everything you need to work remotely," he continued. "Although why anybody would want to spend their time balancing numbers when they don't have to is beyond me."

Tanya lifted the corner of her mouth in a slight smile. "Yeah, well, why anybody would want to run around chasing bail jumpers is beyond me."

"And yet you are doing exactly that right now."

He pulled into a parking slot just in time to glance over and see her widen her smile and shake her head. That smile lifted his heart, made him feel like a million bucks. And the realization that he felt that way scared him. Yeah, he always liked to get a smile or a laugh out of someone, especially a person he was helping who seemed discouraged, but this desire to see Tanya happy was something different. It worried him, because it signaled feelings that could take him down a path he didn't want to follow. There was no point in pursuing a relationship when there was no possibility of them having a future together. They were too different from one another, and they both knew it.

He killed the engine and took a good look around, making sure there was no one lurking or driving nearby before they exited the vehicle.

"This is it?" Tanya said, her tone one of disbelief. She gestured toward the front of the Range River Bail Bonds office directly in front of them.

Danny looked at the window with the company name painted on it. The glass was reflective, making it difficult for anyone to see inside. It was a security measure for the employees, and, in some cases, for the clients.

"There's nothing wrong with it," Tanya quickly added. "It's just that it looks so normal. Like a regular office."

"What else would it look like?"

"I don't know. I guess I imagined some ramshackle building on the edge of town. Or at least that it would be located on a stretch of road out by the county jail."

"We're only a couple of blocks from the county courthouse. That works well for us."

Tanya lifted her eyebrows slightly. "I didn't think of that."

They walked inside and continued past the waiting area at the front. Beyond it was an open area with four desks. Hayley sat at one. She glanced up from her laptop, offered a brief smile, and went back to studying the screen.

Wade stood up from the desk where

he'd been sitting. Jonah Keller, one of their newer employees, also stood. Wade made the introductions, and then they moved to the currently unoccupied waiting area, where they'd have more room.

"So tell me what you've got," Danny said as he sat on the couch. The reason they'd stopped by the office was to see if a possible lead Wade had drummed up this morning was something worth pursuing. Much as Danny wanted to protect and help Tanya, his main professional task at hand was to bring in Victor Durbin.

Tanya sat beside Danny on the sofa, while Wade and Jonah dropped down into the cushioned chairs opposite them.

"My informant says he's seen Victor hanging out with some of the Invaders. They were in a bar having a few beers the other night. Looked like Victor and the gang's leader, Hooper Cantrell, were celebrating something."

"Invaders?" Tanya interrupted. "A guy named Hooper? What's all this?"

"The Invaders are a motorcycle gang," Wade said. He glanced at Danny. "Kind of. In reality, they're more like a group of burglars, drug dealers and petty criminals who like to ride motorcycles. They're a local group. Not part of any of the big national motorcycle clubs. Not as dangerous. At least, not so far."

"So they could provide a pool of people for the attacks on me?" She looked at Danny.

"It's a possibility. I've never heard of any member of their group being a hired assassin. But that could just mean that they're good at it and have never been caught."

Danny watched Tanya hug herself beside him. He was tempted to move closer and wrap an arm around her shoulders. He wanted to do something to comfort her and make her feel better, but that wasn't wise.

"Do you think Victor has joined that gang?" Tanya asked. "Since he's been seen with their leader?"

Danny drew in a breath and shifted his gaze to Wade. They'd had their share of dealings with the motorcycle gang when searching for bail jumpers in the past. "Victor and Hooper sitting in a bar talking and drinking doesn't necessarily mean that Victor is part of the gang," Danny said. "Although if the meeting really did happen, and the informant isn't just making up a story to earn a few dollars from Wade, then I think it's something worth looking into."

"What do you think might be going on?" Wade asked.

Danny shrugged. "I don't know. Maybe Hooper wants to employ Victor to steal cars for the gang to strip down and make money selling parts. Or maybe the two men are simply friends."

"If they're friends, Hooper could be hiding Victor and his accomplice," Jonah offered.

"Hooper's got that house out on Tributary Road," Wade said. "It works as gang headquarters. He keeps a few trailers on the property. Jonah and I could go check it out, maybe watch the place for a while. See if there's any sign of Victor or that other guy, Max."

"If they are hiding Victor there, Hooper's probably got a lookout watching for cops or bounty hunters," Danny said.

"Right. We'll keep a low profile." Wade nodded and turned to Jonah. "Connor keeps some nondescript old cars in the parking lot at the inn. Let's get one of those, drive out to Hooper's place and see what we see."

The two men grabbed their jackets and headed out the door.

"So this is how you do your job a good part of the time?" Tanya mused aloud. "You start with a scrap of information and see where it leads."

"Yeah. The police have all the high-tech methods at their disposal. We go low-tech. We rely on discovering our target's habits and focusing on basic human nature. You might be surprised how often that works."

Tanya turned away from him to look toward the front window and the parking lot. "That gives me an idea," she said, turning back to him. "I think we should talk to the women who went on the trip to Mexico with Dawn. Maybe we'll get some helpful information from them."

"To me, she seemed like the same Dawn she's always been," Barbie, one of Dawn's friends, said as she glanced over to Kathy, who was sitting beside her in the coffee shop.

Both women had originally been slated

to be bridesmaids at Dawn's wedding. After it was canceled, they'd been invited to join her on the trip to Mexico. The third of the would-be bridesmaids couldn't get away from work for this afternoon meeting, so Tanya had already spoken to her over the phone. That conversation had been short, since the woman didn't have any information that could help the investigation.

Making the extra effort to talk to the two ladies who were available to meet in person rather than over the phone had been Danny's suggestion. He'd pointed out that it was easier to read a person, discern if they were telling the truth, if you could see them in the flesh. A phone call—even a video chat—just wasn't the same thing.

"Yeah, Dawn didn't seem any different on the trip," Kathy said, following up Barbie's comment. "I mean, at first, when we met at the airport to leave for Mexico, she seemed a little wistful." Kathy glanced at Barbie, who nodded in agreement. "But who wouldn't be, given that her fiancé had just dumped her?"

"But she snapped out of her funk pretty quickly," Barbie interjected. "She told us she'd rather have a broken engagement than be married to someone who didn't really love her and Calvin."

Calvin. Just the sound of her nephew's name made Tanya's heart ache. She really missed the boy, but according to Dawn, he was having the time of his life in California and loved playing at the beach.

"Did she meet with anybody while you were in Mexico?" Danny asked. "Or have any problems or altercations with anyone you crossed paths with while you were traveling?"

Kathy flashed Danny a wide smile, and Tanya felt a stab of annoyance. She wasn't jealous. She had no reason to be jealous, but it was such an obnoxious, pushy smile.

Tanya glanced at Danny, seated beside her. At his insistence, they had arrived early and taken seats in the farthest corner of the coffee shop, away from the windows and with their backs to the wall. She'd noticed that he shifted his attention to the door every single time it opened, keeping an eye out for the bad guys, as always.

"If you're asking if Dawn was looking for a date while we were on vacation, the answer is no," Kathy said, eyes still locked on Danny. She tilted her head slightly and tapped her chin, showing off her French manicure. "Dawn said she's taking a break from men, getting used to being single again." She stopped tapping her chin and leaned forward toward Danny. "She's not looking for anybody, but I am. How about you? Are you looking for somebody?"

Well, that was just ridiculous given the topic of the conversation. And *rude*.

Tanya crossed her arms over her chest, trying not to glare, not wanting to lose her chance at getting all the information she needed from these two women.

Danny didn't look like he'd even heard the question. He didn't return the woman's smile. There was no flush to his cheeks or extra glint in his eyes. Nothing. For some dumb, unfathomable reason, Tanya felt a spark of triumph over his flat response.

"I'm not looking for anybody," Danny said.

Tanya was surprised at the ripple of disappointment that moved through her. She was glad that Danny wasn't flirting with the woman, but hearing him say so decisively that he wasn't interested in romance had her feeling as if she'd been let down.

"I take back what I just said." Danny directed his words to Kathy, a slight smile on his face. "The truth is I'm almost always looking for somebody, but it's someone I can slap a pair of cuffs on and take to jail."

To her credit, Kathy laughed, and the potentially awkward moment was smoothed over. "Well, then I guess I'm not the person you're looking for."

Beside her, Barbie finished the last of her coffee and reached for her purse. "I'm so sorry to hear about what happened to Calvin and what's been happening to you," she said to Tanya. "I wish I knew something that could help you, but I don't. We went to Mexico, your sister had a great time seeing the sights and shopping like crazy, and after the hurricane hit, we hung out at the resort and still managed to have fun and relax."

"Shopping like crazy?" Danny prompted. "What was she shopping like crazy for?"

"Jewelry, mostly. She bought several nice pieces."

Tanya felt a flare of alarm. That was odd—Dawn didn't have extra money for extravagant purchases. Tanya had actually had to push her a little to spend the broken engagement money on the trip to Mexico since she'd really thought her sister needed a vacation.

Alongside Barbie, Kathy reached for her purse as well. Tanya and Danny stood and expressed their appreciation to the women for their time, and then Dawn's friends left.

Danny sat back down. Tanya did, too.

"I don't know either of those women," Danny said, "but they didn't seem like they were especially nervous or hiding anything."

"I don't know them all that well." Tanya ran her finger around the rim of her coffee cup. "They're Dawn's friends, not mine. But compared to the times I've seen them before, they seemed the same. I didn't feel like they were lying or nervous, either."

"So your sister earns a pretty good income?" Danny asked. "Enough that she could shop for nice jewelry while on vacation?"

"That comment stood out to you, too, huh?" Tanya looked down into the bottom of her empty coffee cup. "She makes decent money selling real estate, but since Calvin was born, she's been careful with her money to save for his future."

"Maybe she had a lot of wedding-cancellation money still left over after paying for the vacation."

"I don't think so. It's not like she and Elliott had planned a terribly elaborate wedding."

"If she had extra money, where do you think it could have come from?"

Tanya thought for a moment, and a couple of ideas popped into her head. This was her sister they were talking about, so she really didn't want to think badly of her. While she and Dawn hadn't always been super close, they did love each other. Tanya respected Dawn for how she'd taken care of Calvin, but it was also true that her sister had been under a lot of stress lately. And she used to be an impulsive, somewhat irresponsible person, especially when she was stressed. Had she gone back to being that kind of person?

"Maybe Joe gave her money hoping to buy access to Calvin," she said. "The other thought that comes to mind is that Elliott gave her access to at least one of his credit cards and a checking account back when they were together. I know that because she told me. Maybe he forgot to officially stop that access when they split up. Maybe Dawn decided to help herself to his credit line and his money." Maybe Elliott really was behind all of this. Perhaps rage over being ripped off by his former bride-to-be was the fuel behind the attacks.

TEN

"We drove by the house on Tributary Road, and it definitely looks like something is going on out there," Wade said as he walked into Connor's office at the inn and sat down. The dark-eyed bounty hunter was the last to arrive for the meeting.

It was early evening, shortly before dinner, and the main members of the Range River Bail Bonds crew had come together to recap the day's events.

Connor sat at his desk. Hayley sat in a club chair next to it. The two of them had spent all day on a new case involving a bail jumper with friends and family outside of the country. It was imperative that the fugitive be recovered before he escaped across the border. Hayley had her gaze fixed on her phone screen as she tapped and scrolled, but Danny knew she was working her case and not just idly checking her social media accounts.

"So what exactly did you and Jonah see?" Danny asked Wade.

"There were at least twenty vehicles parked out there. That's in addition to all the motorcycles you'd expect to see. There were four large travel trailers on the property that weren't there the last time I drove by about a month ago. Several people were milling around outside. More than you'd usually see in the middle of the day."

"The word around town is that the Invaders are aggressively expanding their operations," Connor said. "Maybe they're having some kind of summit meeting."

"Did you see any sign of Victor or Max?" Tanya, seated on the couch beside Danny, leaned forward as if anxious to hear his answer.

Wade shook his head. "Unfortunately, no. But we couldn't really get a good look. There were a couple of guys on the front porch who paid pretty close attention when we drove by. There isn't much traffic out there, so I couldn't turn around and drive by again without them noticing. If Victor and Max are hiding out there, I don't want to risk spooking them and having them move on to someplace else where we'd never find them."

Tanya turned to Danny. "This sounds like something you should tell the police."

"Agreed."

"Since that was as far as we could go with that, I took Jonah with me to check in with some of my informants. Nobody had any useful information. I offered substantial financial motivation. At some point, somebody's going to see something and report it to me."

"Thanks," Danny said. "Tanya and I talked to Dawn's traveling companions, but we didn't learn much, except that Dawn did a lot of shopping while she was in Mexico."

"That's not unusual on a vacation," Tanya said defensively.

"You're right." Danny didn't press the point because he knew Tanya didn't want to believe her own theories, that her sister could have effectively stolen money from Elliott by using her access to his financial resources without his permission after they'd broken up. Or that maybe she'd accepted money from Joe in order to let him see his son and then not given him access to the boy. Either of those men might have hired the fugitives out of anger or in order to get their money back.

"It seems so pointless," Tanya said in a deflated tone. "We're not seeing any results from all this running around that we're doing."

"Sometimes it looks that way for a while." Hayley glanced up from her phone and gave Tanya a sympathetic look. "But then you finally get a break that leads to a capture. Or the cops get the bad guys."

An electronic beep sounded.

"Someone's walking up to the door." Connor tapped the screen on an electronic tablet. "It's Detective Romanov."

The doorbell rang. Danny stood to answer it, but Maribel moved quickly from the kitchen and beat him to it. Moments later, she ushered the detective into the office, where everyone stood to greet her.

"Welcome," Connor said, walking out from behind his desk to greet her. He offered her a chair, and they all sat down.

"So I'm here to ask for a professional courtesy," the detective said. "And I use the term *ask* loosely. Because I'm actually here to *tell* you to stay away from the Invaders."

"Do you have someone working undercover with them?" Wade asked. "Somebody who was at the house and saw me drive by today with another bounty hunter?"

"Something like that. Bottom line, we've got our own operation going on with the Invaders, so you need to back off. Don't drive by the house again, and don't approach anyone in the gang. Just stay completely away from them."

"Understood," Wade said.

"Would you tell us if Victor or Max were staying at the gang house?" Tanya ventured.

"They are not staying there. We're still actively searching for them. We're checking out Joe Flynn's alibis for the three attacks. I also spoke with Elliott Bridger."

Danny felt Tanya's body tense beside him.

"What have you learned? Are you going to arrest either Joe or Elliott?" Tanya asked.

Maribel walked in carrying a tray with glasses of iced tea and passed them out. "Dinner will be ready in twenty minutes," she said to the detective. "There's more than enough if you'd like to eat with us."

The detective took a sip of her tea and then shook her head. "Thank you, but I can't stay long."

"Joe and Elliott?" Tanya prompted.

"Elliott claims he took a mini-vacation. That the breakup with your sister was difficult for him, too, and he needed to get away. That's why he was unavailable for the last few days. He told us his whereabouts at the time of the attacks. He actually came down to the police station to speak with me. I didn't press him hard, because I didn't want him to think he needed a lawyer. A lawyer would likely discourage him from answering my questions. As of right now, I have no reason to arrest him or Joe."

Tanya leaned back on the couch, looking deflated. She'd hoped they were close to having the bad guys rounded up and ending the danger. But she was learning that situations like this were not always quickly or neatly wrapped up. Sometimes unanswered questions lingered for a while.

"Did you learn anything useful from the scene of the parking lot shooting?" Danny asked. "Any forensic evidence that could help?"

"No. We haven't picked up any images from security cameras around the scene that could help us identify the shooter, the driver or the car. Patrol stopped a few vehicles like the one you described, but they weren't connected to the shooting."

The detective took another sip of tea and returned her glass to a nearby coaster. "So tell me, what do you bounty hunters plan to do next?"

Danny glanced at Tanya. "We're going to try to get a clearer look at what happened with Elliott and Dawn before they ended their engagement. Elliott is part of a tech office co-op. We've contacted the administrative assistant there to arrange to meet the members of the co-op at their office. Maybe somebody will be willing to talk to us, and we'll get a lead from there."

"Good idea," the detective said. "That's definitely a situation where someone would be more likely to talk to you than to us. If you learn anything useful, let me know." She got to her feet. "I've got to get going." She offered a general goodbye to everyone and left.

"If Elliott or Joe aren't behind the attacks, then who is?" Tanya said quietly, as if she were speaking to herself instead of expecting an actual answer from anyone. "What do we do if the leads we're all following don't bring us to the answer?"

Danny didn't know what to say. So instead of speaking, he gave in to the im-

pulse to reach over, wrap his arm around
her shoulders and draw her to his side in
what he hoped was a comforting embrace.
The detective's visit had evidently left
Tanya feeling even more worried than she
was before, and he could understand why.
The authorities still didn't have a clear
suspect, so there was no one for them to
arrest. That meant they couldn't do anything to stop future attacks.

*It was just plain old retail therapy. I
bought stuff to make myself feel better.
It all went on my credit cards, and I figured I'd come home and work hard and
pay it off.*

Dawn's words filtered through Tanya's
thoughts the next morning as she grabbed
her purse and jacket and headed back to
the inn's great room. Calvin was safe,
and in Tanya's mind, that was the most
important thing. But apparently, the little guy was getting tired of being away
from home.

At least after a long conversation with Dawn, both Tanya and Danny were convinced that she honestly didn't know what had prompted the attacks and that she wasn't hiding any information from them. And she'd made it clear that she hadn't taken any money or stolen any kind of property from her former fiancé, from Joe, or from anyone else.

Come join us in California, Tanya. I'm worried about you. All those attacks in Range River are horrible. You could hide out here while the police and your bounty hunter friends do their job. Calvin would love it. It would cheer him up. You could stay with us in the room Calvin and I are sharing.

Tanya would be lying if she claimed the offer wasn't tempting. Escaping the threat of danger, the tension and the endless questions that never got answers seemed like a dream vacation right now. But at the end of it all, she couldn't go. For one thing, there was the chance that she would inadvertently lead the criminals to Dawn and Calvin.

Beyond that consideration, she really did believe she was helping the investigation here in Range River. Plus, if she left, the bad guys might just lie low until she returned. Horrible as it was to contemplate, the fact that she was visible in town, potentially drawing them out, might be what was needed to capture them.

Ask me what you want to ask, Tanya. I won't get angry. I haven't done anything wrong or illegal—at least not intentionally. I know you have your suspicions, I know you can't let go of the fact that I made some bad decisions in the past, so let's get it all out now.

That had been Dawn's comment near the start of their conversation. And this morning, Tanya kept thinking about it. It was true that she couldn't forget Dawn's past bad decisions. It was their own mother who had repeatedly said people didn't change, but now Tanya had to wonder if that was really true. She thought of her sister. Thought of the changes in Danny. And the changes in herself. She was getting better at rolling with things and being less rigid, because life was forcing her to.

"Lord, help me understand if people can change," she prayed softly as she continued walking toward the great room. "Is thinking they can't change simply a different form of being unforgiving? Or is it being smart?"

Danny was waiting for her by the front door. They'd already eaten breakfast, but he held travel cups of coffee and offered her one. She happily took it.

"We're taking one of Connor's extra cars so we won't be easily identified," he said. His own SUV had sustained a little cosmetic damage in the parking lot shootout, but having that repaired didn't seem like a high priority for him right now.

He glanced at his phone for a quick check of the outside security feeds before he opened the door and stepped through it. Once outside, he remained alert, scanning the grounds around them as they walked. The crisp fall air had a nip to it, and Tanya zipped up the front of her jacket.

They climbed into a little gray sedan, and Danny drove to Indigo Street. They parked in the corner lot, and as they walked down the wooden sidewalk, they stayed close to the building. The increased tension Danny was feeling was evident to Tanya in his overall demeanor and the expression on his face.

They reached the co-op office. Danny pulled open the door for Tanya, and when she stepped inside, the first thing she saw was Kirby standing behind his desk.

"Good morning," Tanya called out to him.

They had communicated via texts to set

up today's meeting, but they hadn't actually spoken until now. He lifted his brows, a concerned expression on his face. "I can't believe that right after I saw you the last time, somebody actually shot at you."

Tanya raised her shoulder in a half shrug. "Turns out I'm hard to kill."

He responded with a pained smile that was almost a grimace.

"We're here because we intend to find out who's behind the attacks and put a stop to them," Danny said. The hint of humor that Tanya had gotten used to was absent from his voice.

Kirby immediately adopted a more neutral expression. "Of course. Ms. Salazar and Mr. Gibson are already here and expecting you. Let me take you back to the conference room."

"Who else is here in your office?" Danny asked as Kirby led the way down a hallway, past several closed office doors to a large room with windows overlooking Indigo Street.

Kirby stopped beside the oval conference table with several padded chairs surrounding it. "My employers come and go as they please. They did not hire me to give an accounting of their whereabouts to strangers."

"I'm not asking for your employers' whereabouts," Danny said. He sounded calm, but Tanya didn't miss the steely determination in his eyes and his voice. "I want to know that this is a secure scene," he continued. "So tell me, who is in this office? Did anyone show up besides the two people we were expecting to meet with? Is Elliott here?"

Elliott could be here? The thought sent a cold ripple across the surface of Tanya's skin.

"There are no additional people here at the moment," Kirby finally conceded. "Just the two you were expecting." He tilted his head slightly. "Now, if you'll excuse me, I'll let them know you're here." He turned and left.

"Hello." The woman who breezed into the room a few moments later nodded a greeting to Danny and Tanya. She wore jeans and a sweater, had her hair tied up in an attractively messy bun, wore wire-rimmed glasses, and appeared to barely be out of high school. But Tanya knew the sweater was cashmere and the jeans were distressed by hand and likely cost more than Tanya's monthly car payment. Jeannie Salazar had made her first million when she was barely out of high school, and that was nearly fifteen years ago.

"I don't know if you remember me," Tanya said after greetings where exchanged. "We met at Elliott's house when he and my sister were still together."

"Of course I remember," Jeannie said. "That's why I want to help you if I can.

I've always liked your sister. And little Calvin."

"What have I missed?" Clyde Gibson walked into the conference room wearing green khakis and a silk shirt with a bold pattern that appeared to mostly be made up of parrots. "Sometimes it takes me a minute to disengage from my computer when I'm in the middle of something. My apologies if I'm late."

"We were just getting started," Tanya said. On the drive over, Danny had suggested that she take the lead when talking to the co-op members who'd offered their help. He thought Salazar and Gibson might feel more comfortable talking to her and would potentially offer her more information than they would give him.

"We were hoping to talk with you for a few minutes," Tanya continued. "Just to see if you know anything about Elliott or Dawn that might help us figure out what's going on with all of the attacks that have been happening."

"We're both happy to help however we can," Jeannie said, eliciting a nod of agreement from Clyde before everyone took seats around the conference table.

"First of all, I'd like to show you some pictures and find out if you've seen any of these people before." Tanya pulled up pictures of Victor, Max and Joe Flynn on her phone to show them.

"Never seen these people before," Jeannie said after peering at the last picture.

"Me, neither," Clyde said after taking a look.

"How else can we help you?" Jeannie asked as Tanya put her phone away.

At this point, Tanya needed to choose her words carefully. She didn't want to give away too much information about what they knew, whom they suspected and why. They couldn't be certain which side Clyde and Jeannie were on. At this point, she really didn't even know what the sides were. She just knew that there was an organized group of people targeting her—and members of her family.

She took a deep breath. "So there's a chance that the crimes are tied to the tech industry here in Range River," she said. "Or, more precisely, that the criminals we are trying to find are involved in ventures related to technology, and you might have crossed paths with them."

"You do realize nearly everyone has a computer," Jeannie said flatly. "Our smartphones are computers. So anybody, any criminal, could appear to be part of a tech industry if they wanted to." She tucked a few stray tendrils of hair back behind her ear. "Those of us who are into technology are not all hanging out together in the back room of some local computer shop or in our parents' basement. That's some very old-school thinking." She gave Tanya an indulgent smile, as if she thought she wasn't too bright.

"And yet you do gather together here at

various times," Tanya said, gesturing toward the surrounding offices of the co-op.

Jeannie's expression didn't change, but Clyde let out a barking laugh. "Touché," he said with a wide grin. "So what do you want? Computer forensic help?"

Tanya took a deep breath. This was the potentially tricky part. She stole a quick glance at Danny before answering. He gave her a slight but encouraging nod. "Do you know if Elliott's involved in anything shady?" she asked, deciding to go ahead and lay all her suspicions on the table. "Do you know if he's had financial trouble? Maybe he's been blackmailed into using his tech skills to help someone unsavory?"

Jeannie and Clyde both looked taken aback by Tanya's nervously rapid-fired questions.

"No," Clyde said after rubbing his chin and appearing to consider the question for a few moments. "And that's no to all your questions. I haven't seen anything like that. I haven't heard about anything like that. Elliott's always seemed like a stand-up guy."

"I agree," Jeannie said. "And I haven't seen any sign of him having financial problems. He's got that house and the cars. Nice clothes. He and Dawn traveled a bit. He had investors for his projects. From what I see, it looks like he's doing okay."

Or maybe it just looks like he's doing okay.

"What kind of projects is he working on?" Tanya asked. She'd asked Dawn that same question when she'd talked to her last night, but her sister hadn't been able to answer. She'd said she wasn't very interested in his work, and they didn't talk about it much.

"There's no telling what he's working on," Jeannie said. "He put in his time slogging away for other people, and then he made the move to start his own business and develop his own projects. Understandably, he doesn't want to talk about his new endeavors until they're ready to test and he has patent protections in place. He hasn't reached that point yet with the things he's working on."

"Did you witness any animosity between Elliott and Dawn?" Danny asked, finally jumping into the conversation. "Anything that, given what's happened since they broke up, sticks out in your mind? Fights? Arguments? Tension?"

Tanya's stomach clenched as she listened to his question. If her sister had been in a dangerous relationship, she would have said something to Tanya, wouldn't she?

Or would she have been put off by Tanya's orderliness? Her inability to relate to someone with a messy life? Tanya hadn't meant to be judgmental, but had she been? Had her sister been dissuaded from confiding in her because she felt judged?

"Nope," Clyde said. "I was truly surprised and saddened when they called off the wedding."

"Same here," Jeannie said. She glanced at her phone. "I need to get ready for a call." She got to her feet.

Everyone else stood, too.

"Is there anything else you need from me?" Clyde asked.

"No," Tanya said. "I think we're done. Thank you for your time."

As Tanya watched Jeannie and Clyde walk out of the room, she caught a glimpse of Kirby lurking in the hallway a few feet away. How long had he been there? She glanced at Danny. The bounty hunter had already spotted him.

"You heard the questions," Danny said, striding toward the administrative assistant. "What are your responses?"

It looked like Kirby was working up to an outraged denial that he'd been listening, but after a moment, he dropped it. With a more genuine and thoughtful expression, he said, "I've never known Elliott to work with anyone sketchy. But I don't know everyone he works with." He turned to Tanya. "I've also never known him to be unkind to your sister or to little Calvin."

Was he telling the truth? She desperately hoped so.

Tanya and Danny thanked him for his help and left.

"So what do you think?" Tanya asked Danny when they were out of the office and headed for the stairs.

"I think a lot of things. It could be that all three of the people we just talked to were covering for Elliott. It could be that the tech-sounding terminology you overheard was being used in a totally different context, and we're barking up the wrong tree here."

They reached the bottom of the stairs and Danny held the door open for Tanya before stepping outside behind her. "It's possible that some criminal believed Elliott had a lot of money and thought they could get to it by going through Calvin and Dawn," he continued as they walked briskly to the parking area. "Maybe they didn't know that Elliott and Dawn had broken up. That could be where Victor and his connection to the Invaders works in. Maybe they've decided to expand into kidnapping and extortion. Maybe they thought they could kidnap Calvin and get Elliott to pay the ransom. The person you saw in the woods could be connected to them, and now they're after you because of what they believe you saw and heard."

Tanya shook her head. "All of these possibilities are swirling around, and I just want a clear answer."

"At some point, the truth will make itself clear. We just need to be prepared for it to do that with a bang."

ELEVEN

Tanya looked at her chiming phone screen, saw that it was a video call coming from Elliott, and her heart began to race.

She was in the Range River Bail Bonds office with Danny. After their meeting with the two co-op members yesterday, Danny had suggested that they give that visit time to have some fallout. Maybe Jeannie and Clyde would talk to their friends and uncover new information. In the meantime, he wanted to return to basic bounty hunting by checking in with informants, trying to get the names of Victor and Max's known associates, and maybe taking a closer look at Joe Flynn.

Tanya had suggested they go by Dawn's office to speak with her coworkers and see if anything unusual had happened connected to her work. So that was on their list of things to do, as well. Danny had just walked over to say something to Wade when Tanya's phone notification chimed.

"It's Elliott," she called out to Danny, her voice shaking with the rush of adrenaline the call had triggered. Elliott had avoided her attempts to get in touch with him, but now he was calling her. That *had* to mean something.

She tapped the icon to answer. "Hello?"

Elliott's face appeared. Clean-cut, square jawed, artfully highlighted hair slightly mussed as if he'd just run his hands through it. "Tanya, we need to talk."

Danny hurried over and stood beside her.

"I assume you're the bounty hunter friend," Elliott said in a flat tone. "I saw you nosing around my house on my security feed."

"I'm looking to recover Victor Durbin. Do you know where he is?" Danny leaned toward Tanya as he spoke to the screen. Tanya caught a whiff of his sandalwood-scented aftershave. Having him so close, his breath lightly stirring the wisps of hair around her face, was comforting. But in some ways it was also alarming. She was getting so used to having him around. To having conversations with him about all sorts of things—not just about their investigation.

She was going to miss it when this was over and that connection between the two of them was gone. But that was what she wanted. For the attacks to be resolved and her need for protection to come to an end. She wanted to get her life back into a series of neat and orderly patterns. She wanted to return to the organization and sharp focus she was used to.

"I don't know anyone named Victor Durbin." Elliott sighed heavily. "I already told the police that. I can't help you."

"Well, we still want to talk to you," Tanya said in response, floundering for the right words. One of the things she'd learned from Danny was that a short conversation with pointed questions and answers would not be nearly as helpful as something more drawn out and relaxed, where Elliott might inadvertently share a bit of useful information.

She turned to Danny, lifting her free hand in a palms-up gesture that she hoped indicated she was asking what she should do next. Danny grabbed a yellow legal pad and a pen off of Wade's desk.

Another sigh came through the phone. "At first, all of this was just awkward," Elliott said. "Now it's getting to the point where it's bizarre. Look, I broke up with your sister. I know I should have done it sooner, but I didn't. I've talked to the police and sent a text to your sister to let her know how sorry I was to hear about what had happened to Calvin and you. She hasn't responded. Tell me what I have to do to get you and your bounty hunter to stop nosing around the co-op. I'm about to hire a lawyer. This is harassment."

Danny scribbled some words on the legal pad, holding it so that Elliott couldn't see it. "It's not our intention to harass or embarrass you," Tanya said, reading aloud the words Danny had written. "We just want to talk."

Realizing that her own personal connection with Elliott was the most valuable resource she had going for her right now, she glanced away from Danny and his notepad and tried to be her most authentic self. This might be her only chance to get him to talk to her. She and Elliott had had a fairly amiable relationship. She hadn't disliked him until he'd practically left Dawn at the altar.

"Look," she began, intent on sounding conversational rather than as if she were interrogating him—another lesson she'd learned from Danny. "I know you've already talked to Detective Romanov. The police are doing their thing to figure out what's going on and capture the bad guys. Danny Ryan and I are trying something different. More low-tech. We just want to chat with you. Maybe there's some small thing you saw or heard that's more important than you realize. You might be able to provide some scrap of information we could follow up on. Can't you give us a little bit of your time? A half hour, maybe?"

Elliott hesitated for a moment. Tanya fought the urge to put more pressure on him.

"I've got a lot of work to do, but my concentration is going to be shot until I get this over with," Elliott finally said. "So let's just meet now."

Tanya's heart leaped in her chest.

Danny scribbled something again. Glancing down at it, Tanya read the words aloud. "Let's meet at the Range River Bail Bonds office."

"Not a chance," Elliott snapped. "If anybody sees me walking in there, they'll think I'm guilty of something. I'm not going to have my name or reputation tarnished because of this." He paused and cleared his throat. "I'm sorry about what happened to Calvin. He's a great kid. I'm sorry about what happened to you, too. But I'm not responsible for any of this, and I'm not going to suffer the fallout from it."

Danny jotted another note, and Tanya looked at it. "Okay," she said. "We can come to your home. Or the co-op office. Or you can pick a place in town, a café or something. Whatever works for you."

"There's a coffee shop not far from my place, at the foot of the hill. Used to be a convenience store."

"I know it," Tanya said.

"I could use a caffeine break. It's public, but it won't be very busy this time of day. I'll meet you there in thirty minutes. If you aren't there, I'm leaving. And I'm not going to give you another chance. I think I'm being more than fair." He disconnected.

Tanya looked at Danny. "I know the place he's talking about. I got coffee there a few times with Dawn."

"All right. Let's go."

"Want some backup?" Wade asked.

Danny thought for a moment. "It's possible he's innocent, but it's also possible he's offering to meet with us because he's guilty but sure he's way smarter than we are and thinks he can misdirect us and send us off on a wild goose chase. Either way, seeing you hanging around might throw things off. He might get nervous and change his mind about talking to us. It's possible he's done his homework and knows who all of the Range River bounty hunters are."

"So I'll follow you out a few minutes later and stay far behind," Wade offered. "I'll park a couple miles away from the coffee shop. If you need help, you can call the cops, but call me, too. I'll be right there."

Danny nodded. "Given everything that's been happening, we can't be too careful."

Wade turned to Jonah, who was seated at a desk quietly doing some online research. "Okay, kid. You mind the store."

Tanya grabbed her purse and followed Danny out the door to his SUV. Within seconds, they were out of the parking lot and into the flow of street traffic. Danny headed north, aiming for the highway that took them deeper into the hills surrounding town and toward the coffee shop.

"I'm trying to think what to ask him," Tanya said after rolling several possible approaches around in her mind. "The only thing I can think of is to ask if he has any idea of who might be involved. Maybe ask if he knows about Dawn being involved in anything illicit, or if he ever got any weird vibes from Joe."

"All good questions," Danny said.

A green heavy-duty truck came roaring up the highway behind them. It passed them and then got back into the lane ahead of them and zoomed onward. In the last few years, new arrivals from California and the Washington coast had moved into the more remote areas outside town. That led to more traffic. Things were definitely changing.

"Do you want to be the one to question Elliott?" Tanya asked.

Danny shook his head. "He's got no reason to tell me anything more than bare facts, but he's got a personal connection to you. Keep the conversation comfortable and nonconfrontational at the start. That might get him to open up. He might not realize he knows something helpful until he actually says it. Toward the end of the conversation, spring the stuff that might set him off. We'll see if your questions ring any bells for him or make him agitated."

"You mean like nervous?" Tanya asked.

"Yeah. Or defensive. Or just uncomfortable, like maybe he feels guilty or is hiding something."

"Well, he's not hiding right now. There he is." They passed the rural highway's intersection with the road that came down from Elliott's house. Elliott sat in his idling car, waiting to make the turn. Tanya waved. Elliott offered her a lackluster wave in response.

They passed by, and in her side mirror, Tanya could see him turn onto the road behind them.

"At some point, maybe at the transition between the softball questions and the harder ones, we need to show him the photos of Victor and Max and see his re-action," Danny said.

They rounded a curve in the road with a straightaway just beyond it. The coffee shop, not yet visible because of the trees, was a mile or so ahead on the left. Heading toward them was the green truck that had passed them earlier. Tanya figured the driver must have gotten their coffee in a hurry and was headed back to where they'd come from.

The truck drifted over into the wrong lane so that the vehicle was headed directly at them. Instead of correcting, it sped up.

"What's going on?" Tanya asked, horror washing over her. "It looks like the driver's aiming for us!"

"Hold on!"

Tanya shoved her hands against the dashboard, trying to brace herself. Danny jammed the steering wheel hard to the right.

The truck bore down on them. Tanya felt the blood drain from her face, turning it numb. At the same time, fear gripped the center of her chest and clamped down hard on her lungs. At the last moment before impact, the truck swerved and barreled past them. Danny pulled to the side of the road and hit the brakes.

Tanya looked in her side mirror in time to watch the truck barrel into Elliott's sedan. The loud bang from the collision was a sickening sound. It was followed by a metallic screech as the truck pushed the sedan across the pavement and off the road. The smaller vehicle slid out of sight down a grassy, tree-lined ravine.

The powerful engine of the truck rumbled by the edge of the pavement for a moment, then it backed up, straightened and raced away.

Stunned, Tanya finally gasped a breath. Her hands shook as she tried to cross her arms over her chest, suddenly feeling cold and light-headed with shock.

"Call nine-one-one on your phone," Danny said as he worked to get his SUV free of the soft earth and back onto the road so he could drive to the spot where Elliott's vehicle had disappeared.

Meanwhile, using the hands-free device of his SUV, Danny made a quick call to Wade. While describing what had happened to the 9-1-1 operator, Tanya could hear Danny giving Wade a description of the truck and telling him to intercept it.

Unfortunately, Wade had done as directed and had delayed his departure. He was just now making the turn into the hills outside town. There were numerous roads between Wade and the wreck that the truck driver could turn off on to escape.

Danny disconnected the call and hit the brakes at the spot where Elliott's car had been shoved off the road. "Stay here to flag down the ambulance," he said to Tanya as he flung open his door. "I'm

going to see if I can help him." He disappeared into the foliage that covered the
ravine.

The emergency operator continued to
talk, but Tanya didn't register what the
woman was saying. Her mind was focused on Danny. She took one deep
breath and then another, trying to collect
her thoughts. Until an explosion sent an
orange-and-black fireball into the sky.

Elliott's car. She could see flames
through the trees and bushes. Had Elliott
been able to get out in time?

What about Danny?

Tanya practically leaped out of the SUV
and hurried over to the edge of the ravine, calling out his name and waiting
anxiously to hear his voice or see his face,
but there was no sign of him.

"The body was damaged so badly in the
explosion and subsequent fire that it will
be a while before the medical examiner

can offer an official identification." Detective Romanov looked across her desk at Danny, Tanya and Wade, who were seated in her office in front of her. "We recovered the vehicle identification number, which indicates the sedan was registered to Elliott Bridger. You're absolutely certain he was driving the car before the truck struck it and pushed it off the road?"

"Yes," Danny said. "We got a good look at him." He took a deep breath and slowly blew it out, trying to settle the adrenaline still coursing through his bloodstream. To see someone alive and then just moments later see them killed—intentionally... It was not easy to cope with.

"Elliott and I even waved at each other," Tanya added. Seated beside Danny, she reached over to squeeze his hand.

The small scrapes and cuts he'd sustained while clambering down into the ravine stung a little. As did the mild burns—which felt like a sunburn—on his hands and face. But that didn't matter. He was focused on gratitude that Tanya was alive and safe. *Thank You, Lord.* Things could have ended much differently.

The detective turned her head slightly to look directly at Wade. "What can you add?"

"By the time I arrived at the scene, the vehicle had exploded and was sending up smoke and flames. I saw Tanya standing by the edge of the road. Danny came out of the ravine looking a little worse for wear."

Danny glanced over at the friend who was like a brother. Despite Wade's attempt at a joke and the teasing smile on his lips, he knew Wade had been concerned for him.

"I tried to get to Elliott's car to help him," Danny said to the detective. "But the angle of the ground was steep and rocky. The brush around there is pretty thick. I'd just caught sight of Elliott's sedan when I smelled gasoline, and then the explosion happened. I hit the deck at first, then I got up and tried to get to the car to get Elliott out, but the vehicle was already fully engulfed in flames."

Two hours had passed since the event, but Danny could still smell the gasoline.

"You gave the responding officers a description of the truck that caused the accident," Romanov said while tapping a pen on the top of her desk. "But you didn't get a license plate number, and you can't give a description of the driver or say for certain if it was a man or a woman. Is that correct?" She sat back and crossed her arms. "Because I've got to say, if a vehicle is barreling directly at me, I think I'm going to notice something about the driver. And I would expect a professional such as yourself to have at least noted the plate number."

"My priority was to avoid a head-on collision, not take note of the plates or who was driving," Danny said, refusing to let himself get defensive. If he wanted the cop to deal with him as a colleague with common goals, he couldn't afford to let raw emotion or pride get in the way of a thorough postincident interview.

"My general impression was of someone in a tan jacket wearing sunglasses and maybe a black knit cap," he continued. "That's it. After the truck shoved Elliott's car off the road, the driver fled the scene. I wasn't about to chase it down with Tanya in the SUV alongside me."

He took in a breath and commanded himself to calmly blow it out. Maybe he had let himself get defensive after all. He just didn't want the detective to think he was a flake, or that he lacked the initiative to get the most information he could out of a crime scene. With this case, the detective was finally giving him the opportunity to prove that the bounty hunters from Range River Bail Bonds were trustworthy professionals. He didn't want to blow it.

"Let me be blunt," Romanov said. "Because it makes things so much easier when I am." She uncrossed her arms and leaned forward. "My concern here is that you *do* know who the driver was. Maybe it was the bail jumper you're trying to recover, and maybe you want to find him on your own so you can earn your recovery fee." She spared a quick glance at Tanya. "If the police recover a bail jumper, there is no recovery fee paid to the bounty hunter." She turned back to Danny. "Or maybe you aren't motivated by money here. Maybe you're out for revenge and think you have the right to dispense justice."

Danny fought to contain his rising level of frustration. He couldn't let her accusations get the better of him. She was outlining all her concerns. He needed to be equally straightforward so he could lay those concerns to rest. "Range River Bail

Bonds does pretty well for itself," he said. "Missing out on any individual recovery fee is not going to break us financially. That said, I take my work seriously, because dangerous people shouldn't be running around on the streets."

He paused to take a calming breath. "As far as revenge or passing out justice goes, let me just say that I don't want to become like the people I'm chasing."

Maybe what he'd said was too simple, but after studying him for a moment, the detective gave a slight nod.

"Okay," Romanov said as she turned to Tanya. "How about you? What did you see?"

Tanya clasped her hands in her lap. She appeared about to speak, but then her face reddened and tears formed in her eyes. She pressed her lips together and shook her head as the tears began to fall. Danny's heart ached to see her so miserable. She'd been through so much.

She sniffed loudly and sat up straight. Tears rolled down her cheeks, but she wiped them away. "All I saw was the green truck barreling toward us and then speeding away after it hit Elliott's car and shoved it off the road."

"The timing of the event is pretty remarkable," the detective said. "The truck was at the exact place it needed to be to take out Elliott. Who else knew about the meeting?"

Tanya shook her head. "It all came about quickly. We didn't have time to tell anyone other than Wade. Jonah Keller, one of the employees at the bail bonds office, was there. So he heard about it, too. I don't know who Elliott might have told."

"We'll interview Jonah," Romanov said. "Meanwhile, do you have any gut instincts on who might be behind the attack?"

Tanya shrugged.

"We were at the office co-op yesterday talking to a couple of members, Jeannie

Salazar and Clyde Gibson. Maybe it was somehow connected to that," Danny said.

The detective jotted down the names.

"Joe Flynn comes to mind, too," Danny said. "The truck that hit Elliott had been modified. It had a stronger engine than the one that comes standard with those kinds of trucks—you could hear it. And the front grille wasn't factory-issue. It looked heavier and had no trouble shoving Elliott's car off the road."

"I'll check in with Joe Flynn," the detective said. "See where he's been today. In the meantime, I want you two to stay away from him and his shop."

Danny nodded.

"Of course," Tanya said softly.

"When you talked to Elliott's friends at the office co-op, did they mention anything helpful? Did they happen to mention if they knew of any animosity between Elliott and Joe? Or Elliott and anybody, for that matter?" Romanov focused on

Tanya. "Or maybe between Elliott and your sister?"

Tanya shook her head. "They both made it sound like everything was fine between Elliott and my sister up until they canceled the wedding. I'm not sure if I believe that in light of all that's happened. Also, just to fill you in on everything we learned, they claimed they didn't recognize photos of Victor and Max."

The detective sighed heavily. "Yeah, well, sometimes people don't want to get involved, so they'll deny knowing anything."

"Do you think today's attack could have come from someone involved in that motorcycle gang, the Invaders?" Tanya asked.

"We'll check into that. Now, I've got to get going. There are quite a few people I want to talk to." She stood, indicating the meeting was over and they were dismissed.

As Danny followed Tanya and Wade out

of the police station, his thoughts lingered on the day's events. Clearly, the driver of the truck had targeted Elliott. The assailant must have had information, resources and the ability to implement a plan with very short notice. That meant the Range River bounty hunters were facing an opponent even more formidable than they'd realized.

He watched Tanya as she walked ahead of him to the SUV, praying that he would be able to keep her safe.

TWELVE

"Thanks for offering to help, but I've gotten everything taken care of." Maribel Fast
Horse stood in the inn's great room wiping
her hands on a dish towel. "The beef stew
has another twenty minutes to go in the
slow cooker. The rolls are on the baking
sheet, ready to pop into the oven. Iced tea
is brewed. You two relax. Figure on eating dinner in about forty-five minutes."

"The stew smells great," Danny said.

"It does," Tanya agreed. "And I'm starving."

"I'm glad you're hungry, because I made
a lot of it." Smiling, Maribel turned and
walked back into the kitchen with the
dogs trailing behind her.

Danny and Tanya were at the inn sitting on a sofa in front of the fireplace. It had been twenty-four hours since their conversation with Detective Romanov. After the emotional jolts of yesterday, Danny had thought it would be best for Tanya to have a quiet day at the inn. He still wanted to make progress in the case, so earlier in the day, he'd suggested that Tanya reach out to Kirby again to see if anyone in the co-op would be willing to talk with Tanya now that Elliott had been murdered. Perhaps Elliott's death would prompt someone who'd been hesitant before to speak up now.

Kirby had agreed to help, but so far he hadn't reported any responses. That was a disappointment. But at least Tanya was safe and sound at the moment, and that was the most important thing. Despite Danny's best intentions to not let it happen, he had developed significant personal feelings for her. She was a smart, strong, loyal woman with a generous heart. He'd seen evidence of that as she'd taken care of her nephew, tried to be understanding with her sister and done her best to keep her cool, all while assailants were trying to kidnap or kill her or people around her.

Danny's romantic relationships in the past had all been short-lived. Truth was, in each instance, he'd felt like he was playing a role. He was overly conscious of saying and doing the right thing. When he was with Tanya, he felt like he could be his own genuine, hyperaware, mildly restless self. She was okay with that. Feeling the warmth of her acceptance had opened his heart wider than he'd ever imagined possible. Maybe wide enough for him to risk telling the control-freak accountant how much she'd started to mean to him.

It was unsettling to realize that he had no real reason not to follow his heart. There was nothing to keep him from taking the chance, telling her how he felt and seeing how things rolled from there.

Well, nothing except for the reality that they needed to get this current case wrapped up before the two of them could have anything like a normal life. And there was the possibility that he'd misread the situation and she wasn't romantically interested in him at all.

Tanya's phone rang. "It's Kirby," she said before tapping to answer and then putting the phone on speaker. "Hi, Kirby, have you heard from anyone?"

"I sent out the texts this morning asking for people to talk with you, and no one responded. Then a few minutes ago, I got a reply from one of the co-op's founding members, Nikki O'Hara. Have you ever met her?"

"No, I haven't. But Elliott mentioned her name."

"She's hosting a get-together at her home tonight for the other co-op members. She's very upset about what happened to Elliott. We all are." Kirby sighed deeply. "She wants you and Danny to come."

"Why would she want us to come?" Tanya asked. "If she's willing to talk to us, wouldn't it be better to do that someplace other than the middle of a crowd?"

"She said there are several co-op members who might want to help with the investigation, but they don't want to talk with the police. They're afraid it will bring them negative publicity, or they might look like suspects. They're hiding behind their lawyers, and Nikki's annoyed about that. She wants to help, so she sent out invites for this get-together, describing it as an occasion to grieve Elliott's passing together, and also to talk about how it might affect the co-op going forward. She says if you show up, she'll talk to you. And if the others see that, maybe they'll go ahead and talk to you, too."

"Is this a dinner?" Tanya asked.

"More like a cocktail party. Starts at seven. If you arrive early, you can interview her first, and then she'll introduce you to the other members as they arrive."

Tanya gave Danny a questioning look.

"Send the address," Danny said toward the phone.

"Doing it now," Kirby responded.

Tanya's phone chimed, and she tapped the screen to see the address. "That's out by the southern edge of town," Danny said, looking over her shoulder.

"It is," Kirby confirmed. "It's a nice house centered in a patch of forest. I'm heading over there now to help get things set up." He drew in an audible breath and blew it out. "Elliott didn't deserve what happened to him."

"No, he didn't," Tanya said. She'd had to break the news to her sister. Even though Dawn had been angry with Elliott, she'd still been heartbroken to hear about how he was killed, and she'd burst into tears at the news.

Tanya thanked Kirby and ended the call.

"I'll go to this get-together," Danny said. "You stay here. Relax. Enjoy dinner."

If one of the other bounty hunters had been around, he probably would have had them tag along. But Wade was assisting Connor and Hayley on a stakeout, and Jonah didn't have enough experience to be helpful in this situation.

"Should we tell Romanov about this?" Tanya said.

"I'll send her a text. Though she'd probably be more interested in hearing about it after the fact, when we have something useful to tell her. Hopefully that will be the case."

"I'm going with you," Tanya said.

Danny opened his mouth to argue, but Tanya held up her hand before he could speak. "My reasoning is the same as it's been from the beginning. There will be people there who have seen me before. Or who at least met Dawn when she was still with Elliott. They'll be more relaxed around me than they will be around you, which means they might reveal more."

"Huh," Danny said. "Do you realize you're starting to sound like a bounty hunter?"

She lifted the corner of her mouth in a half grin. "Like a bounty hunter with an organized mind full of logic and reason."

"True, and that's good. The problem is you don't have the skills and training most bounty hunters have to keep themselves safe when things get dangerous."

The expression in her eyes turned serious. "I realize that, but the reality is that things are already dangerous."

She was right, of course. But that didn't do anything to ease the anxious knots forming in Danny's gut. He and Tanya might just engage in a few harmless conversations tonight, but situations could change in an instant. One of the co-op members could be directly connected to the attacks. Danny and Tanya could end up having to do more than just talk.

A tall privacy fence lined the road in front of Nikki O'Hara's house, but the heavy gate had been left open.

"I hope we learn something that will get us moving in the right direction," Tanya said as Danny slowed to make the turn onto the property. *Please, Lord*, she added silently.

Danny drove through the gate. The driveway, lined with planters filled with river rocks and evergreen shrubs, split into two branches. One segment led to the left toward a six-car garage. The other segment led slightly to the right, culminating in a loop in front of a sleek single-story house. The sun had just set, and light spilled from the edges of several curtained windows.

There was only one car in sight. Presumably, the residents of the house parked in the garage. Tanya guessed that the inexpensive compact car in front of them belonged to Kirby. "Looks like we're here ahead of the guests," she said.

"Good. Maybe we can get our interview with Nikki out of the way without interruptions before anyone else arrives." They parked and headed for the house.

As they got closer, it became obvious that the front door was ajar. Danny hesitated at the threshold, so Tanya stopped alongside him. He glanced up at a security camera and gave a slight wave.

"What are you doing?" Tanya asked.

"Just trying to show that I do have decent manners."

No one came to the door, so a moment later, he knocked on it, pushing it farther open. "Hello?" he called out. "Ms. O'Hara? Kirby?"

He stepped through the doorway, and

Tanya followed him. Bluesy, coffee-house-style music played farther back in the house. There was no one in sight, and they headed down the white-tiled hallway side by side. Tanya caught the scents of beef and fried potatoes. Her stomach growled as she and Danny reached a glossy white kitchen, where Elliott sat at a butcher-block island. He held a gun pointed directly at her. An electronic tablet, a phone and a fast-food burger with a pile of French fries dumped onto the wrapper beside it lay in front of him.

"Thought you'd never get here," Elliott said with a cold smile. Then his gaze flickered to Danny. "If you try to do something heroic, bounty hunter, I will shoot you. Now, come on into the kitchen. Slowly."

Elliott stood while they moved toward him. "Stop," he said, when they were still a few feet away. "Give me your gun," he said to Danny. "Don't pretend you haven't got one. And hand over your phone." His gaze flickered to Tanya. "I want your phone, too."

Shocked beyond words that Elliott was still alive and standing in front of them, Tanya slipped the purse strap off her shoulder and began to dig around inside for her phone. Elliott impatiently grabbed her purse before she could retrieve her phone and tossed it onto the countertop. He held his hand out to Danny and tossed the bounty hunter's gun and phone on the counter, as well.

"Where's Nikki O'Hara?" Tanya asked hoarsely. "Is she here in the house?" Those were the first questions that came to mind as she tried to make sense of what was happening. Was Nikki the mastermind of the attacks? Could she have helped Elliott fake his own death?

"Nikki is at her main residence in Seattle."

"If you broke into this house, you must

have triggered some kind of security alert," Tanya said. "I'm sure the cops are already on their way."

"Oh, I don't think so. Nikki gave me her password a few weeks ago when I wanted to return something I'd borrowed from her while she was out of town." His cold smile morphed into a superior smirk. "When I used the password to get into the house today, I was wearing a wig and a hat and carrying a mop and a bucket. I made sure I didn't look directly at the camera as I came in through the front door. When she got an alert that someone was in her house, she believed an employee from the cleaning service she uses had dropped in to do some work, and she wouldn't think twice about it.

"After that, it was easy enough to disable the cameras inside the house. Nikki will probably just think it's a hitch in the system." He smiled and appeared to be waiting for acknowledgment of his genius. That was possibly why he was taking the time to explain himself.

Tanya itched to wipe the self-satisfied smirk off his face, but her brain seemed stuck on making sense of the situation. "So Nikki didn't really arrange a get-together tonight? She didn't contact Kirby?"

"Nope." Elliott shook his head. "Most of us have multiple numbers and social media accounts related to our businesses. Fooling Kirby with a few messages was not that hard."

"You're not dead," she said, feeling stupid as soon as the words came out. He had a few marks on his face, some scratches and reddish burns, probably caused by a triggered airbag. They were not the severe burns she would have expected following the crash she'd seen and the explosion afterward.

Elliott shrugged. "It's not that hard to hire someone to stage a car crash," he said.

"But there was a body inside your car."

"A sad soul I found panhandling to buy booze the night before. I simply gave him a big bottle of the hard stuff and let nature take its course."

So the night before Elliott contacted Tanya, he'd already planned the crash and obtained a body to make it look like he'd been killed. He'd arranged everything. The thought that he could be that cold and calculating was chilling. Even more terrifying was the fact that this evil man had nearly become Calvin's stepfather.

"You won't get away with whatever it is you have planned," Danny said. "Forensic tests will prove that the body in the car wasn't you. The authorities will come after you."

Elliott nodded. "But by the time they do, I'll be long gone."

"You're telling us all of this because you intend to kill us," Danny said matter-of-factly.

A chill raced across Tanya's skin.

"Yes," Elliott said. "That's exactly right."

"Why?" Tanya asked. She'd been shocked when she first saw Elliott and realized he was pointing a gun at her, but her initial numb curiosity was wearing off, and stark fear was taking its place. Her entire body began to tremble. "You and I always got along okay. Just a few short weeks ago, you were going to marry my sister. Why are you doing all of this?"

"I don't dislike you, Tanya," Elliott said in a tone that was all the more unnerving because it sounded so calmly conversational. "This isn't personal. The fact is that you two have been relentless in your investigation and I won't feel like I can make a clean escape until the both of you are dead. Once you're dead, I'll stage the scene and have the cops chasing some imaginary killer while I quietly slip out of the country."

Tanya's body began to tremble harder,

and she moved to wrap her arms across her stomach.

"Hold still!" Elliott stepped toward her and lifted his gun so that it was pointed at the center of her forehead. "Don't you do anything until I tell you that you can."

She looked over at Danny. His attention was fixed on Elliott.

"Why are you doing all of this?" Tanya asked, returning her gaze to Elliott. As long as Elliott was talking, he wasn't shooting. And as long as he wasn't shooting, there was still hope that Danny would come up with a plan to save them.

"I took investment money to develop some online scamming software. After it was done, and I realized how much money I could make if I kept the program myself, I decided to do just that. I also decided that I didn't want to share my newfound fortune with a wife and a stepson. Nor did I want to give the original investment money back."

"Do Victor Durbin and Max Curry work for you?" Danny asked.

"No. The people who hired me to write their scam software hired those two clowns to try to force me to hand over the code. After I managed to elude them, they apparently decided to try and get to me through Dawn. Obviously, they weren't aware that I'd broken up with her. I can only assume that they went after Calvin figuring that he would be a good bargaining chip to force his mother to tell them how they could find me. I've been staying away from my house and all my usual hangouts since I decided to keep the code for myself."

Elliott sighed heavily. "Now, it's time to wrap this up, because I have things to do. Get moving. We're going out back." He used his gun to gesture toward the end of the kitchen that opened onto a dining area. "That way. Tanya first. I'll be right behind the both of you. If either of you makes any unnecessary moves, I'll start shooting."

On shaky legs, Tanya started walking. The dining area opened onto a living room where a sliding glass door had been left open. She could see a bluish glow of swirling water with steam rising above it out on the patio. It took her a moment to realize it was a hot tub.

"Keep moving," Elliott said after she'd slowed for a few seconds.

Tanya passed a couch and saw something heaped on the floor on the other side of it. Not some*thing*. Some*one*. *"Kirby!"* He was beaten and unconscious but still breathing. She saw his chest rise and fall. Tanya reached toward the injured man.

"No!" Elliott snapped at her. "You stand back. Your bounty hunter friend is going to pick him up and put him in the hot tub."

"He'll drown!"

"That's the point. I need him out of the way. He really thought Nikki was holding a party at her house tonight until he got here and saw me. I can't have him telling anyone that I'm still alive. And if the bounty hunter refuses to do as I say, I'll shoot you. And then I'll shoot him. And then I'll shoot Kirby."

Tanya risked a glance at Danny. This time, he was looking at her. He shifted his gaze to the open sliding glass door and then looked back at her. He did it a second time, and she realized what he meant. He wanted her to run out the door.

She couldn't possibly just save herself and forget about the repercussions for Danny. He wasn't planning on letting himself get shot, sacrificing his life for hers, was he? She couldn't let him do that.

She thought of the man she'd come to know over the last few days and realized that giving up was not the way he rolled. He must have a plan. She'd seen the confident and determined expression in his eyes. But what was the plan? What was he going to do? And what was *she* supposed to do after she got through the door?

If she got through the door.

The need to know every single thing, every step of the plan, took over her thoughts. For several excruciating seconds, she was paralyzed with indecision and anxiety.

"Pick up Kirby and dump him in the hot tub. *Now!*" Elliott snapped at Danny.

Danny looked at Tanya, and she nodded to indicate that she understood what he wanted her to do.

He winked at her in return, and she almost burst into tears. He turned and bent down as if to pick up Kirby while at the same time yelling, *"Go!"*

Tanya ran. She was out the door, past the hot tub, off the patio and into the dark, forested backyard of the property faster than she'd ever moved in her life. She heard exchanges of gunfire and shouting behind her, but she didn't dare turn to look back. Fear set her heart hammering even faster as she ran, and soon she couldn't catch her breath.

Realizing she was in danger of tripping and falling, she dropped down behind a tree. Panting for breath, she looked toward the house. The living room lights had gone out. She could still see the eerie glowing light from the hot tub and she could hear the slight gurgle of the water, but there were no more gunshots. And no voices.

What had happened? Was Danny still alive? And where was Elliott?

The sounds of footsteps and snapping branches shot sparks of fear up her spine. Especially when she realized they were coming from behind her. She spun around as a hand clamped over her mouth.

Danny.

He dropped to the ground beside her. "We need to be quiet," he whispered while looking back toward the house. He removed his hand, and she followed his gaze. Elliott's outline was etched by the bluish light from the hot tub. He stood with his gun in his hand, facing the grounds where they were hiding, his head moving from side to side as he looked for them.

She turned to Danny and saw the small gun in his hand.

"My backup," he whispered near her ear. "Because despite what you think, sometimes a solid plan can fall apart. You have to be able to think on the fly."

Really? He wanted to revisit that debate *now*?

A sudden gunshot made her jump. The glass door behind Elliott broke apart, and he dived for cover. Confused, she turned to Danny. The sound of the gunshot hadn't originated from beside her.

"Someone else is out here trying to shoot Elliott," he whispered. "Hopefully, one of the neighbors heard Elliott and I shooting at each other and has already called the cops. Meanwhile, we need to get moving."

"Wait." Tanya placed her hand on his arm. "We don't know where Elliott went, and we don't know where the shooter is. Shouldn't we just stay hidden?"

The sound of someone moving in the forested backyard and getting closer gave her the answer. They *had* to move. Then she heard a second set of footsteps from the opposite direction, also getting closer.

Danny was already half-crouched and ready to run. Tanya tried to match his quick response, but fear and uncertainty over which way to go made her feet heavy and her movements fumbling.

Elliott appeared out of the darkness in front of them and forced them to stop. He pointed his gun at Tanya. Danny pointed his gun at Elliott.

"I just popped in a full clip of ammo," Elliott said to Danny, apparently not realizing that there was at least one other shooter out there. "How many rounds do you have left in that little six-shooter? None, I think." He pointed his gun at Tanya while still talking to Danny. "But even if you do have bullets left, as soon as you fire at me, I'll fire at her. Now, start walking back to the house. You *are* going to dump Kirby into that hot tub."

What? Elliott was still focused on drowning Kirby? Didn't he realize that someone else out there in the darkness was trying to kill him? Did he think Danny had fired the shot that had shattered the glass door behind him?

Another gunshot was fired from the darkness. This round came from behind Elliott, striking him in the shoulder and causing him to spin and stumble.

As soon as he fell, Tanya spotted Victor in the woods a few paces away. The kidnapper turned his attention, and his gun, to Tanya.

Danny grabbed her arm and pulled her along with him as he started running.

"Get ahead of them!" she heard Victor call out to someone. He had to be talking to his thug partner, Max. That meant that even with Elliott down for the count, there were still two criminals hunting for them in the darkness.

"*Do* you actually have any bullets left?" Tanya barely managed to gasp out the words to Danny as they ran.

There was a moment's hesitation before Danny answered, "No, I don't."

Dear Lord, help.

She heard sirens.

"Cops!" Victor yelled.

"We've got to get out of here, now!" Max hollered back.

There was the noise of footsteps and breaking branches, but then the sounds began to fade. The criminals had changed directions. Instead of chasing Tanya and

Danny deeper into the forest, they were headed back toward the house.

"What are they doing?" Tanya asked as she and Danny slowed down and then stopped. "Why aren't they running farther into the woods to get away?"

"If they try to escape into the woods, they'll be tracked by a K-9 in no time. They're probably trying to get to a car or truck they left parked around here some-where."

"If they're able to escape, the attacks on me could keep happening," Tanya said flatly. "Because the man I saw when they kidnapped me in the forest must have been one of the tech investors who hired them to get Elliott. The only way they can protect his identity and keep him out of jail so they can get paid is by getting rid of me."

"You're right," Danny said grimly. "I won't let those two get away. You stay here."

"No! I'm coming with you." He'd done so much for her. She wasn't about to let him try to stop the bad guys on his own. "Let's go," she said, managing to sound braver than she felt. "We're wasting time."

Danny started to track the fleeing kidnappers, and it was quickly evident they were headed for the garage. As he and Tanya drew closer to the building, they heard a vehicle start up behind it, and a pair of headlights flicked on in the darkness.

"How are we going to stop them?" Tanya asked. She and Danny were on foot, and the criminals wouldn't think twice about driving over them. Danny still had his gun. He'd tucked it into his pocket, but it was useless without ammunition.

"I know," Tanya said quickly. "Let's close the gate!"

Danny shook his head. "Too far away. They'll be out and gone before we get over there and shut it." He looked around, and his gaze seemed to snag on the smooth, decorative river rocks that lined the driveway.

Bang!

A shot came from behind them. Tanya spun around to see Elliott staggering toward them. The moonlight revealed the blood on his shoulder where he'd been shot. She could also see the angry, vengeful expression on his face. Her lungs tightened in fear.

Elliott held his gun at his side. It appeared he was having trouble staying upright, but he gritted his teeth in determination as he lifted his gun to fire it at her.

Danny moved to step between her and Elliott. He might be willing to take a bullet for her, but she wasn't going to let that happen. As Danny got closer, she reached for the gun handle sticking out of his pocket. She was surprised by how heavy it was. Nevertheless, she hefted the thing and flung it at Elliott, hitting him smack in the middle of his forehead. He went down like a ton of bricks.

Behind them, Victor and Max were already barreling up the driveway.

"Quick, get Elliott's gun!" Danny yelled.

Choking down a fit of squeamishness, Tanya scrambled toward Elliott to take the weapon out of his hand. She could hear the criminals' car engine roaring up the driveway. She wasn't going to be able to get the gun in time for it to do any good.

She heard cracking sounds behind her, one after another. She snatched the gun from Elliott's hand and spun around in time to see Danny standing in the driveway flinging river stones at the car that was almost upon him. Shatterproof glass held the windshield together, but a spiderweb of cracks crisscrossed its surface.

Whichever thug was behind the wheel steered hard to the side to avoid another rock, and the small sedan's right-side tires went off the edge of the driveway, getting caught in the planter alongside it. The driver was able to right the vehicle, but the mishap had slowed him down just enough for a cop car to make it in through the gate, putting a stop to the thugs' escape.

THIRTEEN

Several more patrol cars followed the first, all with their blue and red lights flashing.

The first officer out of his car glanced at Danny, who pointed at the kidnappers' sedan, yelling, "Victor Durbin and Max Curry!"

With guns drawn, the police quickly swarmed the vehicle. Tanya watched as Victor and Max were taken to the ground, hands cuffed behind their backs, while police frisked them and searched their car. Finally, the two thugs who'd started everything by trying to kidnap a sweet little boy were placed in the back of separate patrol cars.

Victor glanced in Tanya and Danny's direction before being driven away. Tanya thought he looked defeated. She felt a wave of relief, but at the same time, she was still concerned. Victor, Max and Elliott had all been stopped before they could cause more harm, but what about the people who'd financed them? How would she and Danny stop the people who'd put up the money for Elliott's original malware project? Would they still come after Tanya because she'd seen one of them when she'd been kidnapped in the forest?

She drew a deep breath, prompting herself to focus on and appreciate the blessings that had already come her way rather than looking for reasons to worry. *Thank You, Lord, for Your protection*, she prayed. *And please help the authorities find the criminals who prompted all these horrible actions.*

"You're still holding Elliott's gun," Danny said to her quietly. "Let's set that plus my backup gun on the ground and step away from them. Cops are understandably nervous if they see civilians walking around with guns at a crime scene."

As soon as they'd put distance between themselves and the weapons, Danny called out to the closest cop, Officer Billings, to let him know the firearms were there. "Elliott Bridger is right over here." Danny directed the patrolman toward the grassy patch of ground where Dawn's former fiancé, still unconscious and unmoving, wasn't so easily visible in the darkness.

Billings radioed for an ambulance.

"You'll need two ambulances," Tanya interjected while Billings was still talking to dispatch. "A man named Kirby Heath is inside the house. He's unconscious. I don't know the extent of his injuries."

Residual adrenaline still coursed through Tanya's veins. It left her feeling shaky and oddly detached from the situation. Most of the officers appeared to know Danny, and the sergeant who assumed control of the crime scene asked the bounty hunter for details about what had happened. When Danny finished recounting the events, the sergeant asked Tanya if she had anything to add.

"No, nothing," she said, suddenly very tired. So much had happened in the nine days since Victor had first showed up at her house pretending to deliver a pizza. Had that really been just over a week ago? It felt like the ordeal had been going on for so much longer.

"Detective Romanov is going to want to talk to you later tonight or tomorrow to get your official statements," the sergeant said, his glance taking in the both of them.

"Of course," Tanya said.

Danny nodded. "Anytime."

Because the house was a crime scene, Tanya and Danny were not allowed back inside. They stood on the driveway and watched as two ambulances rolled in through the gate. One headed toward the house, while the other was directed to Elliott.

Tanya kept her attention on the EMTs that went into the house. A short time later, they came out with Kirby. The co-op administrative assistant had regained consciousness, and he called out to Tanya as his gurney was being rolled toward an ambulance.

She walked over and followed alongside as the EMT pushed him toward the emergency vehicle while a paramedic kept a watchful eye on his vitals.

"I thought there was going to be a cocktail party here tonight." Kirby's voice was weak, and he sounded confused. "I thought Nikki would be here. But I only saw Elliott. And then..." His voice trailed off as tears began to flow from the corners of his eyes. There were red marks, cuts and scrapes where it looked like he'd been struck on the side of the head. "I thought I was helping solve all the horrible crimes that have been happening," he finally resumed. "I thought I was going to help catch Elliott's killer."

Tanya placed her hand atop his and squeezed. "It's okay, Kirby. I believe you. I know you were trying to do the right thing." She was very sorry for the sense of betrayal he must be feeling. He'd thought Elliott Bridger was his friend and that he could trust him. Her family had thought Elliott was trustworthy, too. So much in the world was uncertain, and no matter how hard she tried to plan the path of her life, there was no getting around that simple fact.

The EMT working with Kirby loaded him into the ambulance, and they left for the hospital.

Danny, who'd been talking to one of the

officers working the scene, walked over to Tanya. "Are you all right?" he asked.

She nodded, telling herself that she *was* all right. She wasn't injured like Kirby. She was fine. But she didn't feel the sense of triumph she'd expected to feel now that the criminals—at least the ones she knew of—were locked up. The big players behind it all were still at large.

She tried not to let her thoughts linger on that and tried to focus instead on the good things she'd seen while going through this horrible experience. The law enforcement officers and emergency medical workers who'd showed up to help. The family and friends who'd called or sent her messages of support. The group of bounty hunters who'd taken her in and treated her like family. And the fact that her sister and nephew were safe and sound. She wanted to be grateful instead of worried, but right now that was a hard thing to do.

Danny stepped up and wrapped his

arms around her, holding her close to his chest. She let herself relax into his embrace and be comforted by his strength. Danny didn't seem to be in a hurry to let go of her, which was nice. More than nice.

He loosened his embrace, and when she looked up at him, he leaned down for a kiss. The press of his lips and the intermingling of their breaths stirred up feelings of belonging and happiness that she suddenly realized she'd been craving for a very long time.

It was an emotion both new and strangely familiar, a feeling that seemed to warm and fill her heart.

A feeling that might be...love?

Could she really have fallen in love with wild Danny Ryan? A *bounty hunter*? That had certainly not been part of her life plan. And she'd thought that she could never be with someone who made his living in such a dangerous profession. But she'd seen for herself how competent he was. And what a positive impact he made on the community by doing what he did. Maybe it was time to toss those old plans aside and give in to her impulses and see what happened.

After a moment, she started to giggle.

Danny pulled back. "What's so funny?"

"Big, tough bounty hunter." She laughed harder. "You caught the bad guys by throwing rocks at them. Rocks!"

"I do whatever it takes. And I don't stop until I get what I'm after." He flashed her a teasing grin.

Suddenly, her laugh died out, and her breath caught in her lungs. She was struck by the realization of what it would truly mean to let her guard down and open her heart to Danny. She could potentially get hurt. Badly. But what was the alternative? Did she really want to go back to the way she'd been living her life—always playing it safe?

Fear moved through her like a ribbon

of cold air. She'd allowed herself to care deeply about Danny and had gotten used to his company. Yet she had absolutely no control over where their relationship might go. It might not go anywhere. What if she was misreading the situation? What if he was still the same old flirtatious Danny Ryan that he'd been when he was younger, and his kiss meant nothing at all?

She took a couple of steps away from him, unable to stop the worries flickering through her mind. She definitely needed to spend some time thinking and praying about what she should do next.

"Victor Durbin is singing like a canary." Detective Romanov took a seat in Connor's office at the inn. One of Connor's cats, a tortoiseshell named Layla, jumped down off a bookcase to sit in front of the detective and stare at her. Danny was just about to walk over and pick up the feline when, to his surprise, the detective patted her legs and the cat jumped up to settle in her lap.

"You don't have to let her sit with you if you don't want to," Connor said.

"She's a pretty stubborn cat, though," Wade chimed in while Hayley smiled and nodded in agreement. "If you push her off, she'll probably sit at your feet and stare at you until you let her back up."

"She's fine." Romanov scratched the top of the animal's head. "Victor was the first to offer information in return for lesser charges," the detective said, returning to the topic at hand. "So the district attorney is giving him the plea deal. Max Curry still isn't talking. Elliott has already lawyered up. He knows he'll be looking at murder charges before long. We're still in the process of identifying the body he used to fake his own death in the crash, but we're already building that case." As Romanov spoke, she rubbed the cat's ears, and it almost looked like the animal smiled.

Danny got the feeling that the formerly aloof detective had declared an end to giving the Range River bounty hunters the cold shoulder. Or at the very least, she was warming up to their pets.

"What about Elliott's financial backers?" Tanya asked in a concerned tone. "Do I still need to worry about them coming after me because they think I saw one of them when I was abducted outside Aunt Winnie's house?"

Danny glanced at Tanya seated beside him. In the roughly twenty-four hours since the arrest of Elliott and the two hired thugs, Tanya's demeanor had run the gamut from relieved to happy to nervous and back again. He didn't blame her. A lot had happened in the last ten days. He hoped she'd allow him to help her through the emotional fallout that she seemed to be working through.

She'd chosen to stay at the inn last night and again tonight while a security system was being installed in her home. She was fearful that Elliott's criminal patrons might still come after her. Everyone was worried about that. As long as she remained at the inn, the rest of the team would stay here, too.

"Victor gave us the names of the two men who hired him and Max to kidnap Calvin," the detective said. "They were the same people who gave Elliott the money to develop his malware program to steal credit card data. Both of the financial backers have now been arrested. The feds already had them on their radar for other credit card data theft activities, so they'll be taking over the prosecution of that aspect of the case."

"Does this mean Joe Flynn and the motorcycle gang, the Invaders, have been cleared?" Tanya asked.

"Yes and no. Joe has strong alibis for

when all of the attacks occurred, and we can find no direct link between him and Elliott or anyone else connected to the case, so he's cleared. We believe the driver of the green truck who helped Elliott stage the crash is a member of the Invaders, so we're still working on that. Victor has admitted that he met with the gang's leader, Hooper Cantrell, because they wanted to hire him to supply them with stolen cars."

When the detective finished speaking, Danny offered up a silent prayer. He hadn't liked the idea of Tanya moving back into her home without her case completely wrapped up. Not even with the excellent security system installed at her house. He'd already imagined himself camping out in his SUV in her driveway every night to make sure she was okay. But it appeared that he wouldn't have to do that, because now she was finally safe.

He turned to Tanya as she exhaled a deep breath and smiled at him. He smiled back. He wanted to continue looking after her. Not because she couldn't take care of herself, but because he wanted to do things for her. Make her life easier. Make her happy. He wanted to see her smile. Every day.

It was good that the danger was over, but he didn't want the two of them to go their separate ways now that the case was settled. He didn't think his heart could take it if he didn't continue seeing her on a regular basis. The connection that had formed between them was something special, and he didn't want to let it go. She'd made him stronger. And he hoped he'd done the same for her.

"I need to get going," Romanov said. She gave the cat a couple more head scratches before lifting her off her lap and setting her on the ground.

"I'll see you out," Danny offered.

Tanya went with them, expressing her thanks. They ended up walking the detective all the way to her car. Night had fallen, and as Romanov drove away, the red taillights of her car glowed in the darkness.

Danny looked up at the stars overhead. They appeared especially bright in the cold, black sky. Winter would be coming soon, and when it was covered with snow, Range River would look very different than it did right now.

"It feels good to be outside and not have to worry about someone trying to kill me," Tanya said.

Danny turned to her. Her expression was the most relaxed it had been since he'd showed up at her house the night of Calvin's abduction. She also looked like she had something on her mind, and he was afraid she was going to tell him good-bye.

"Do you want to walk around the grounds a little now that it's safe for you to do so?" he asked, trying to forestall the inevitable.

"Sure."

Nervous energy twisted his midsection.

He'd likely blown any chance of a relationship with her when he'd impetuously kissed her. He was sure of it now. He had given in to the emotion of the moment, hadn't stopped to think it through, and he'd made things awkward between them.

They walked past the edge of the inn's parking lot and onto a dirt path that wound between towering pines and eventually headed toward the river. Moonlight reflected on the surface of the steadily flowing water.

Danny didn't want to say goodbye. And he didn't want things to be awkward between them. They were good together. He knew it. Maybe he just needed to say it. Say how he felt, and hope she'd tell him she felt the same way, too.

"Look, I'm just going to lay everything on the table," he finally blurted out, coming to a stop and turning to her. "I have never met anybody like you. You're smart and funny and a little obsessive-compulsive, but that's okay."

"Thank you." She smiled a little shyly as she tucked a few tendrils of hair behind her ear.

Her smile fanned the ember of hope in Danny's heart into a bigger flame.

"You're beautiful and loyal, and when I wake up every morning, I look forward to seeing you during the day," he continued, the words pouring out as if a dam had broken.

He wasn't completely certain, but he thought he saw tears start to pool in her eyes. Did that mean he should shut up or just keep going? Might as well keep going.

"If you don't have room in your life for me as anything other than a friend, I'll make that work," he said, though he wasn't sure he could do that. The truth was he'd fallen in love with her. He didn't think of her as just a friend. "I won't try to kiss you again if you don't want me to," he said, though kissing her was something he really, really wanted to do. "I didn't want to fall in love with you, but my heart went barreling ahead of me, and, well, here we are."

"Here we are," she echoed. Except when she said the words, she sounded much more confident than he had sounded. She took a step closer to him. "We're both here. Together. And I'm so glad you didn't let me fall in love alone."

She rose up on her tiptoes and kissed him, and he bent down to meet her. Their lips touched, and in an instant, Danny felt all his past heartaches heal and all his current doubts vanish. Everything he'd been through in his life had been worth the effort and the pain just to be able to reach this moment. He wrapped his arms around her and pulled her closer.

They were two people meant to be together. Two hearts meant to beat side by side. Danny had found what he'd really, truly been searching for, and he would do everything he could to be the man Tanya wanted and needed.

Eight months later

Tanya swayed to the mellow music, her cheek pressed against Danny's broad shoulder as he held one of her hands in his and rested his other hand on the small of her back. Her heart was full, and she was so very grateful for the life she'd been given. They danced beneath the latticed covering on the patio outside a lovely Italian restaurant on the banks of the Range River near Indigo Street. Tiny white lights twinkled in the wooden slats overhead and in all the other places where they'd been threaded throughout the patio. The lights had even been wrapped around the potted plants. Hayley and Maribel had done a very nice job with the reception decorations.

The May wedding had been held at Still Waters Church, which was where the Ryan family attended services. It was where Connor had gone when he'd first adopted his siblings nearly twenty years ago and hadn't known what to do next. He'd just known that his brother and sister needed a better life than the one they'd had growing up.

"I love you," Danny said softly in Tanya's ear.

She squeezed his hand. He'd been saying that on a regular basis for months now. She knew she'd never get tired of hearing it. "I love you, too."

"Look!" Calvin shouted, shoehorning himself between the couple and holding up a box with a picture of an outdoor bowling game on it. "I won this!"

"That's cool," Danny said, bending down to take a closer look.

Tanya glanced over at Maribel and Aunt Winnie at the far end of the patio. They'd set up games to keep the little kids occupied and had stacked up plenty of prizes so every child would go home with something.

"Whoa!" Dawn called out, tracking down her son. "This is their special day, sweetie. Let's leave them alone. Why don't we take a little walk and go look at the river?"

"He's fine." Danny swooped up his new nephew and gave him a noisy kiss on the cheek. "You did an outstanding job as ring bearer, buddy."

"Danny and I have already had our first dance, plus a couple more," Tanya said to her sister. "I think we can put the formalities aside now. It's time for everybody to cut loose and have some fun. And that includes my favorite nephew." She reached out to rub his hair and to admire that little tuft that always managed to keep standing up no matter what.

"It's still your day," Dawn said. "Your romantic evening. And you deserve so much happiness. The both of you."

Dawn began to choke up with emotion, and Tanya laughed at her. She couldn't help it. And she didn't try to hide it. The events that had started with the kidnapping all those months ago had brought the sisters closer together. Tanya would never have chosen for the attacks to happen, but with the passage of time, she'd been able to notice the blessings that had come out of those terrible experiences. The warmer relationship with Dawn was one example. Her new bounty hunter family was another.

While Dawn worked on convincing her son to head back to the games at the other end of the patio, Tanya glanced around at the friends and family dancing nearby, sitting at the tables enjoying the food or hanging around with Maribel and Aunt Winnie while they played with the kids.

As she scanned her surroundings, Tanya's gaze snagged on Joe Flynn. Dawn and Joe were working on putting their hard feelings from the past behind them and building a relationship that would make life better for Calvin. They might not ever be a romantic couple again, but at least they would be friends. They'd even started taking their boy to church, because they realized their goal was too big for them to accomplish alone. They needed faith to make a seemingly impossible task possible.

As Dawn led Calvin away, Tanya turned to her new husband. Circumstances had forced her to step out of the carefully constructed life she'd lived and do things she'd never imagined she could. She'd stepped out in faith, because what else could she do? And look what had happened—all kinds of good things.

She felt a smile form on her lips.

Danny smiled in return. And then he winked.

Tanya winked back before leaning in for a kiss. Spending her life with this man was going to be an adventure full of unexpected surprises. And she was looking forward to it.

* * * * *

Dear Reader,

"God creates all kinds of people for all kinds of reasons. Just because someone gets on your nerves doesn't mean there's something wrong with them. Perhaps they are exactly the way they are supposed to be."

Years ago I heard a pastor make that comment during a Sunday School lesson and I've remembered it ever since. It reminds me to take a deep breath and be patient when I'm getting frustrated with someone.

Some days I take a lot of deep breaths!

Danny Ryan is an example of someone with a personality type that caused him a lot of problems when he was growing up. But later in life, he discovered that the qualities that were a problem earlier had become assets that helped him excel at his job.

The world truly needs all kinds of people. I hope you had fun tagging along with

Danny and Tanya and getting introduced to a few of the residents of Range River, Idaho. Next up will be a story centering on Danny's sister, Hayley. Like all of the other bounty hunters at Range River Bail Bonds, she knows how to track down trouble.

I invite you to visit my website, jenna-night.com, where you can sign up for my newsletter mailing list. You can also keep up with me on my Jenna Night Facebook page or get alerts about upcoming books by following me on BookBub. My email address is Jenna@JennaNight.com. I'd love to hear from you.

Jenna Night